E T E R N I D A D

CIMMERIAN RISING

B. THOMAS HARWOOD

HERSCHEL-FLOYD PUBLICATIONS

PRESENTS

E T E R N I D A D

CIMMERIAN RISING

Original Story By B.Thomas Harwood
Copyright © 2012-2013

Cover Art By Kyle Anderson
www.kyleanderson.com

For my brothers Gregg & Gregg

One through blood

One through avocation

For your faith

For your friendship

For believing

TABLE OF CONTENTS

PROLOGUE

No one knows where he came from. No one witnessed his birth. No one knew of any woman who carried him, or of any man who claimed to father him. He simply appeared one day from the undergrowth of the South American jungle in the land that today is known as Venezuela. He promised food to the starving, peace to the factions at war, wealth to the impoverished, and hope to the forlorn. But they were all of them, victims to his charming beguile.

With a simple touch of his fingers upon the flesh of those he met, they were instantly mesmerized and bound to him. He kept his face masked, save for his chilling dark eyes, and anyone who dared look directly into them ultimately met the same fate as those he had touched. Those that followed him and served under him, whether by their own will or not, had no memory or recollection of life before *Jeringas Mortifer*.

It was said he was the direct offspring of Morbus, one of the Primeval Scourges of the continuum, which made Jeringas Mortifer an immortal extension of his alleged sire. It was also said that in the early stages of his rise to power, Mortifer was aided by an assortment of seemingly unnatural beings and beasts, whose origin may forever remain a mystery.

Legends grow, as they always do, and as legend would have it, Mortifer predated the Chavin civilization of Norte Chico, which would have made him around 2500 years old at the point in time where this tale begins.

While the European empires squabbled over territory rights, Jeringas Mortifer seduced, tricked, and enslaved untold thousands into his service. One by one, every man, woman, and child within his expanding territory had either fallen under his spell, or perished under his rule.

The most capable fighting men he assimilated into his ever growing collection of armies and naval squadrons. Many more were sent deep into the mines to collect precious metals and stones; the currency that drove Mortifer's empirical machination. The rest became farmers and herders and cooks and laborers of the various sorts necessary to maintain Mortifer's occupied lands.

Whether it was due to age, physical limitation, or even moral disagreement, any who failed at their assigned task were first publicly tortured and then brutally executed. Not even the children were exempted from this rule.

By the time the empirical powers of Europe even began to hear rumors of his existence, it was too late for any of their leaders to do much about him. Mortifer's forces had grown so large and become so deeply entrenched in the southern hemisphere of the New World that it was virtually impossible to assault his Caribbean fortress in Caracas.

The European powers had their sights and resources fixated on the disputed territories to the north. As such, they remained largely unconcerned with an unrecognized ruler over a mostly undeveloped region. He was a problem that most of Europe was convinced could be quashed later in time.

So, Mortifer continued to seize the lands and the very souls of the people who lived among them. From Lake Maracaibo all the way to the Orinoco River delta, he was allowed to reign there unopposed and unchallenged. Aiding his legitimacy in the minds of many, all of this was *supposed* to have transpired, at least according to one legend.

While Mortifer's shadow cast an ever growing shroud over the South American mainland, another legend was unfolding at the same time.

At the very fringe of the territories under European control, the small island settlement of Camahogne underwent a power transfer of a different kind.

Populated almost in its entirety by people of African descent, Camahogne had recently overthrown her minority ordinance, freed every sugar plantation worker from slavery, and redistributed its lands to her people. When news of their accomplishment spread throughout the Leeward Islands, it rocked the established orders all the way from Caobana to Kairi and Bella Forma.

Like Camahogne, the vast majority of the inhabitants who lived on Kairi and Bella Forma were plantation slaves of African heritage. Once word of Camahogne's independence reached there, the relationship between the Spanish plantation owners and their slaves began to simmer. It was an uneasy existence at both ends of the whip.

Before long, the few remaining Spanish military outposts began to vacate by sea to the north. For they knew, that eventually the simmering would reach its boiling point. Without the backing of the Spanish military, the civilian slave owners were left with no choice but to abandon the islands entirely.

Despite their close proximity to the mouth of the Orinoco, and their wealth of fertile, developed plantation land, Jeringas Mortifer had long refused to cross the narrow strip of water known as the Dragon's Mouth to invade the islands of Kairi and Bella Forma. As far as conquest was concerned, the islands should have been easy pickings for him.

By this time, they had little military resistance, no hope of reinforcement, a population that was already accustomed to the barbarism of slavery, and virtually every sovereign neighbor to the north simply *expected* Mortifer to take the islands at some point.

It was unlikely that any of them could or even would risk opposing him. Why he had not invaded Kairi and Bella Forma was the subject of an ongoing debate among the island colonies of the Lesser Antilles, all of whom grew more nervous with every mile Mortifer's reach extended.

Some said it was simply the name of the strait that made him wary. Others pondered whether his territory had already amassed to such a point that further expansion would stretch his forces too thin, or perhaps his maniacal aspirations had been temporarily placated.

Fewer knew of the stone tablets, carved by the ancient Arawak people - tomes that had been recently found by men still enslaved as they tilled the soil of Camahogne. Fewer still knew what any of the ancient scripture actually meant. Once word of the slave uprising reached his citadel, Jeringas Mortifer began to gather his suspicions, and what he suspected was enough to give him pause, to make him carefully consider his every next move.

While the recently liberated inhabitants of Camahogne raced to hide the only known interpreter who could translate the passages, and Jeringas Mortifer calculated a means to capture both the translator and the tomes of the lost prophecy, on the tiny island of Statia, a local fishing boat captain hurried home to witness the birth of his son.

EVERY STORY HAS A BEGINNING

WELCOME TO THE WORLD OF

ETERNIDAD

CHAPTER ONE

THE LUNAR PROCER

A swift wind and smooth seas made for enjoyably fast sailing beneath the clear blue sky. It was early July, a bright and hot summer day, one that was typical of the days which came right before the rainy season. But for Captain Pieter Thomas of the *Vissen*, this day was anything but typical.

For this day, his wife was expecting to give birth to their first child. He had only half a day's catch stowed beneath the forward deck of his vessel. It was hardly enough to make the trip from shore worthwhile. However, returning home and little else was all that mattered to him.

Captain Thomas stretched his considerable hands out for a moment. First, he inspected his palms, then the weathered skin that covered his knuckles and the backs of his hands.

They were the hands of a sailor, a fisherman, and a life long laborer. He was a broad shouldered man in his middle thirties, of average height, with mild blue eyes and dark brown hair that seemed impervious to the effects of the sun. His forearms and biceps looked something like thick mooring lines spun from granite. The muscles slid effortlessly back and forth when he opened and closed his grip. As he looked over the effects of his many hard years at sea, Captain Thomas thought he heard a voice calling from behind.

"Come again?" he inquired.

"What do you think it will be?" asked Franklin, the captain's first mate, who was manning the wheel of their ship. "What do I think *what* will be?" Captain Thomas inquired in reply.

"The little one! Do you think it will be a boy or a girl?" Franklin asked once again. Captain Thomas studied his first mate for a minute as well.

Franklin Smit was nearly ten years older than Pieter, slightly taller, and slightly thinner. His previously blonde hair had been bleached completely white by his many years at sea. His skin, once light and mild, had become tanned like leather. Every fold and every crease in Franklin's face seemed so exaggerated compared to when Pieter first befriended him.

"A boy, I think it will be a boy!" Captain Thomas replied again.

"What makes you say that? You haven't been talking to that fortune teller, have you?" Franklin returned with a chuckle. Captain Thomas shook his head and smiled humorously.

"You know I avoid that crazy woman like the plague. No Franklin, the tides favor a boy, and my heart tells me so." Franklin nodded, smiled in return, and slowly began tacking the wheel.

"What do you make of the slave uprising on Camahogne, Captain? Some are saying the violence will spread, that another uprising is inevitable. One more revolt could squeeze every slave holding island from the mainland to Caobana into chaos. I fear those people. I fear they will do to us what they did to their masters. What is your take?" Franklin inquired.

Captain Thomas stared up into the canvas of their 47 foot dogger and pondered the words briefly. "I don't know what there is to be afraid of, Franklin," the captain began.

"They are just people. People, like you and I." Franklin stared back in disbelief.

"Pieter, they are not like you and I. They are savages! They used sickles and machetes and all sorts of farm tools to hack down their masters. They killed the very men who employed them." Captain Thomas' eyes narrowed as he turned to face his first mate.

"You have a strange sense of what it means to be employed, Franklin. Take us, for example. I employ you. But you are free to leave at any time. I came halfway around the world, and you followed, but we both did so of our own free will. And while we were young and eager to escape the ever changing rulers and borders of our homeland, we were both afraid if you recall. Afraid to end up lost at sea. Afraid to leave the motherland behind, war torn as she may be." Pieter paused for a moment.

"Now imagine these men, these *savages* as you call them. Imagine what they must have felt, dragged from their homes in the middle of the night. Beaten, and whipped into submission, and then lined up like livestock. Or perhaps like the fish that we catch, put out to market and sold to the highest bidder. Imagine being piled into those dark, dank ships, and taken thousands of miles from home. Set to sail over rolling seas in a big wooden box with masts, terrified and trapped, not knowing a thing of what is to come, unable to see the light of day. Imagine feeling nothing but the weight of their iron shackles in the darkness. Imagine yourself in their place. Imagine being taken from your wife, or worse, watching her die because she contested you being taken from her. Then imagine seeing your daughter sold for the purpose of breeding, or your son fetching a fair price for his strong build. Ask yourself, how much of this could you stand before you fought back, before you turned crazed and wild, before you became... *savage*?"

"Enough!" Franklin shot back. "Captain, you don't need to lecture me on the slave trade. I have seen more than enough to understand its evil. I have seen so much that I do not have to *imagine* much at all." Captain Thomas shook his head.

"I know, Franklin. But it does beg the question. Who among us are the savages, really?"

"Did you know the fate of those who were not armed, and surrendered? It could have been worse. The blacks spared them, the women and children too, Franklin. Turned them all over to an English soldier, a young man by the name of Tyre. He ferried them off Camahogne to a Portuguese outpost on the island of Barbados. And then the strangest thing of all happened." The captain glanced forward to check their heading while Franklin waited for him to continue.

"This Tyre fellow, he went back. Presumably to stay with the blacks."

"Stay with them, you say? Whatever for?" Franklin asked.

"Nobody knows. They have been calling this Tyre fellow a hero for saving all the lives as he did. It's been speculated that he returned to stay with the freed slaves as a condition for the release of the Spanish captives. But that seems an odd explanation. After all, the slaves allowed him to leave in the first place. It's not as if the British are the best of friends with the Spaniards these days," the captain answered.

"Aye, and it's a good clip from Camahogne to Barbados, around 150 miles one way, give or take. I don't see any man forced into captivity getting that far away only to return. But he is British, you said. Only the Brits can understand the thinking of another Brit." Both the captain and his first mate burst into laughter at the comment.

Captain Thomas breathed in through his nose, slow, and deliberately. There was barely a passing cloud anywhere on the horizon. The scent of misty seawater filled the air every time the hull of the *Vissen* cut through another wave. It was, indeed, a perfect day for sailing. Which, in the mind of Captain Pieter Thomas, made it the perfect day to become a father.

"I'll tell you the real madness of this New World, Pieter," Franklin began, interrupting his captain's private thoughts.

"It lies to the south of us. That crazy king, Jeringas Mortifer. From the way the locals on the mainland would have us believe, he controls the entire coast of Venezuela. And from there, all the lands between the coast and the banks of the Orinoco river. I don't know what to believe. He sure has all of the mainlanders worked up. The Caribs and the Arawak, living and working together, for him! Who could have guessed? And the Muisca tribes from the west, the isolationists, even they have joined in under his service. And then there are the tribes from further into the mainland, some for which we have no names yet. He claims that he is some sort of god, and the tribal folk believe it! His followers may be primitive, but they number in the thousands, perhaps tens of thousands, and when they work together it is said they can literally move mountains." Captain Thomas chuckled.

"My dear Franklin. If you believe all that then you're just as gullible as the primitives. Men moving mountains. Ha!" Franklin smiled knowingly.

"I have not been there, but they say high up in the mountains, on the Pacific side of the mainland, there are stone towers that can touch the sky. The sky, Pieter! Made from the very stones that once made the mountains themselves. Maybe they are not so primitive after all." Franklin smiled even wider as he imagined the sight of stone towers touching the clouds.

"Yes, and it seems that every week another Spanish expedition goes looking for the golden city of El Dorado, only never to be heard from again. I think your head has been baking in the sun too long. Speaking of which, you must make sure the sun is still touching the sky when we get home. With your slow hands at the helm, it will be nightfall before we reach shore. Speed us along, Franklin. I have a son to welcome into the world!"

As the captain reached for the wheel, Franklin took to hauling the lines and manipulated the sails so they could gather as much velocity as possible.

A million different things went racing through Pieter's mind. He had hoped to be better prepared for the arrival of his first child. He and his wife had all the necessities to greet a newborn baby.

They had shelter, a crib, plenty of linens and food, and a reliable midwife was already in their employ. What troubled him was the not so distant future.

There was very little in the way of schooling available in their remote part of the world. *Books*, he told himself, *I need to acquire books.* Pieter considered a good education of far greater value than any amount of currency. *How long will the peace hold out?* he asked himself.

Pieter always believed that more of Europe was coming. He was a Dutchman himself. While much of Europe quarreled over territory rights and boundaries back home, there in the middle of the Caribbean sea, it seemed all of Europe was well represented, and living together in peace.

Spaniards numbered the greatest. But there were nearly as many English, French, and Portuguese settlers. Less common were the Germans and Italians, with some Danish, Dutch, and a few Swedes thrown in for good measure. They all got along just fine, alone on the edge of the new world.

Trade was the common denominator that bound them. Without peaceful trade, the very existence of the island settlements would have been in peril. They all relied on one another to survive, and no matter their linguistic differences, gold coins, regardless of origin, all spoke the same language well enough.

Each island was unique in its cultural and geographical make up. Some were largely flat, and well suited for raising livestock. Others were dome shaped, like a circular beach surrounding a single hilltop or mountain peak - the remnants of volcanoes that had long been expired. Every island produced a crop of some kind, even if just enough to offer some sustenance to its own inhabitants.

Some were dedicated to sugar cane, a hugely profitable export back to Europe. Coffee was another big income earner in the region. Others grew simple grain which rarely, if ever, left the Caribbean. Even the more mountainous islands were dotted with trees that bore exotic fruits such as avocado, grapefruit, balata, guava, bananas, papaya, barbadine, star fruit, coconuts... too many to list by name.

Every man, woman, and child was a farmer, or gardener, or harvester on some level. However, no single island produced enough of anything to be completely self sustained.

Pieter often pondered why life was so simple in the New World when compared to the one they left. It took anywhere from two to three months to cross the Atlantic. Ships from Europe carrying supplies were few and far between. So, when left to their own devices, without the interference and persuasions of their kings and queens and politics, when given no choice but to get along in order to survive, it seemed the people of the islands did precisely that. They got along. They survived.

How do I explain all this to my little one? Pieter thought privately. *And what will we do if this Mortifer character should come for our lands and our homes?*

Pieter had no desire to return to his birthplace in Amsterdam. He had enough of war, enough of monarchs squabbling, enough of it all, long before he ever made the voyage to the place he now called home.

He was not the most religious man in the world, but he was born a Christian, and he knew how to pray. Every day, Captain Thomas prayed that more of Europe would come.

While he cared not for their politics, he knew how valuable a greater military presence could be given the prospect of Mortifer's expansionist nature.

He put little stock in the legends and whispers of ancient tongues that began to chatter about him more and more frequently. He certainly didn't believe that Mortifer was a god, or any kind of immortal.

He believed him to be a fanatic and maker of war, both attributes of flesh and blood, of man. Yet the whispers grew louder with each passing day.

People he once considered reliable and unflappable were beginning to pass along the most far fetched accounts of Jeringas Mortifer and his supposed deeds.

Just as he reached up to wipe a bit of sweat from his brow, Captain Thomas flattened his hand to block the bright sunny rays. Land was fast approaching, and a whole new chapter of his life awaited him there.

Franklin made haste to the bow of the boat with a mooring line in hand. His wife, Dorothy, awaited their return at the edge of the dock. Dorothy was neither slim nor robust, and though just a few years younger than Franklin, her face showed little of his age.

Her eyes were bright blue, both kind and thoughtful looking. Her hair was somewhere between brown and blonde, which alternated in tightly curled strands. To Pieter, she was a welcome presence, as Dorothy had already successfully birthed two girls and a boy of her own.

While Franklin fastened the mooring lines, Pieter dumped a couple buckets of sea water in the fish pen, a sort of on-board live well he devised to keep fish alive and fresh right up to their eventual sale or entry to the smokehouse.

"Come on Pieter, the fish will be there for later. Your wife's water broke not half an hour ago. It is time."

Dorothy's voice matched her eyes well; kind, thoughtful, and in that moment, a steadying calm.

With a hand on his ship's rail, Captain Pieter Thomas swung himself over the side in one fluid motion, landing hard but square upon his feet. He walked swiftly and with purpose to the beach.

As he reached the trailhead that was barely visible amongst the tall grasses, he made it a point in his mind to remember as much of the day as he could. From the bright blue skies to the refreshing breeze that carried the fragrance of a hundred thousand colorful wildflowers in bloom all around him. His mind's eye carefully captured and recorded everything that was happening as the day went on.

Native birds sang in harmony as he traveled further inland. When he passed by the village square, he saw a young girl alone on a bench, strumming her lyre. There was a complete absence of chatter, as most of the adults were out working the fields near the quill to the south. The young girl took no notice of Pieter as he strolled past, and Pieter would have paid her no mind except for her welcome addition to the symphony of sounds that filled the air and lifted his spirits.

Pieter's home was a little further inland from the village square, just as he preferred, and exactly in the place he chose to build it. The building itself was a little more elaborate than the wood frame homes that most commonly dotted the island.

It was a single story house built in the traditional Dutch fashion, but with an old fashioned thatch roof. As it was, the house would not have looked out of place in his original home city of Amsterdam.

Pieter built his home between two massive trees that kept the house well shaded and cool enough in the sweltering July heat. Perhaps most importantly, he built the house near a small waterfall that was fed by a natural spring. This spring provided fresh water year round, from on high near the summit of *weinig berg*, or little mountain.

The spring fed creek ran in the rear of the house, where Pieter had spent countless hours arranging the flattest stones he could find into something of a courtyard. It was here that Lauren, his wife, lay stretched out on a padded tumbona, with Cilla, the midwife, at her side.

Pieter swiftly stepped across the courtyard and knelt at his wife's side, and carefully took her fingers into his grasp.

Lauren was breathing slowly, and methodically, as if she had put herself into some sort of meditative trance. Her eyes cracked just slightly at the touch of Pieter's hand, and she smiled at him for a brief moment.

Neither of them said a word.

Pieter was probably the more nervous of the two, even though they had both rehearsed the event in their minds many times over. He took a deep breath to steady himself, and silently looked upon his wife. Lauren was half a year shy of thirty, but as Pieter saw her, she had not aged a day in their nearly six years together.

Her skin, once milky white, was now a buttery light tan. Her hair was long, shiny and perfectly black. Her eyes were wide and blue, as blue as the Caribbean waters that surrounded their tiny island paradise. But even as sweat gathered upon her brow, and she was railing against the kind of pain that no man could ever really understand, she had never been more beautiful to him.

"Your timing was just right. Any moment now, it will begin," said Cilla. "Just keep her hand in yours. Lauren and I, we'll do the rest," Cilla added confidently, as Lauren nodded quietly in agreement.

Cilla was a farmer's wife, nearing fifty years of age, and a veteran of at least a dozen births. Her hair was equal parts brown and gray, her eyes were a dark brown, focused and wise.

Her skin complexion was tanned and weathered, for she too had spent her share of time in the sun with the farming crews. She was thin, but strong for her size, and quite capable of drinking any man under the table.

Pieter felt Lauren's hand tightening around his own. For the next thirty minutes, Pieter just kept to himself, and remained as quiet and composed as he could. He cringed at the torment and agony in his wife's precious face. The sounds of her labor echoed off walls of their home and the rocky outcropping behind them. Cilla softly and steadily coached Lauren each step of the way. Before long, Cilla announced she could see the baby's head.

"One more good push, Lauren, and we're all done here," Cilla said, almost joyously. Lauren gathered herself with a long, deep breath, and in one sharp moment, her baby was born.

Cilla quickly got the baby breathing, and in an instant, they all heard the baby's first cries as he opened his eyes to the world. Cilla gently swabbed the newborn's head with a fresh, damp cloth, and handed him over to Lauren.

"It's a boy!" Lauren exclaimed.

"I knew it would be," Pieter quietly gushed, with an overdue exhale of relief. His wife was now the mother of his child, and his eyes grew misty at the sight. It was the greatest beauty he had ever known.

Pieter was surprised at how quickly their son calmed, his cries were tamed to a series of coos and whimpers almost immediately. Before long, Lauren found herself crying as well, but she was crying the purest tears of joy.

"He is so beautiful!" Lauren exclaimed in wonder.

"That he is, dear," added Cilla.

"Look, Pieter. He has your eyes. So serious already. Look at them drifting about, like he is already memorizing the layout of the yard," said Lauren, as her own tears dried away into subtle laughter.

"And, if he is anything like his father, he is already making plans to improve the place," added Cilla, laughing along them both. Pieter beamed with pride, and found himself chuckling with joy at the spectacle.

"He is certainly daddy's little man," said Pieter. His eyes followed those of his son as they looked about. Pieter laughed to himself at his own hidden humor, for just as he made it a point to remember every detail of this special day, here was his son, as fresh from the womb as could be, already mimicking him.

Cilla clipped the cord and continued cleansing both the newborn and mother alike.

"You certainly seem to know who Mommy is. It's as if you already recognize her!" said Cilla, as she wrapped the baby in fresh linen.

"How about you have a look at your daddy while I help Mommy get to feeling better. What do you say to that?" asked Cilla, her voice growing playful and loud. The baby cooed as Cilla gently handed him off to Pieter.

"Hi there," Pieter began softly, as his baby stretched out his little hands to touch Pieter's face.

"I am your father. Want to have a look around?" Pieter stepped lightly upon the stones that led to the creek's edge. There he stood for a while, holding his newborn, whose eyes were transfixed on the little water fall pouring into the crystal clear pool just a few feet away. Pieter's son let out a brief "Aye-yuh!" and then pointed to the waterfall.

"You like that?" Pieter asked, as he knelt down to the water's edge. His son just smiled in wonder at the gentle rush of falling water, and the refreshing mist that it carried to both of their faces.

"It's water, see?" asked Pieter, as he cupped his hand to collect a sample. "Pure water. It's the stuff of life," Pieter added, just as he let a few drops trickle on the baby's head. The water ran down the baby's face and collected near his upper lip, which he promptly blew back upon Pieter's cheek.

"Ha ha, very funny. I can already see you're going to be trouble, little one," Pieter said sarcastically, while his son erupted into little baby giggles.

Pieter grabbed another handful of the cool water and splashed some on his face. He then shook his head to spray some water back upon the boy. Pieter let his lips and his cheeks hang loosely, which made a burbling sound the baby found especially humorous.

Pieter was so fascinated by his newborn boy, he could barely even hear Cilla calling to him.

"Oh Pieter! Quit hogging the baby. Mommy wants to see him again."

Just another moment, Pieter thought to himself. As he looked upon his son, and then to the stream, and back to his son, an idea was born.

"Coming," he answered at last. Pieter then briskly returned to his wife's side, his little one seemingly in awe of the rapid pace at which his father could move about.

"I think we should name him Stephen, for I believe he will grow up to be a man of great strength," said Pieter, as he handed the boy back to his wife. Cilla eyed the child for a moment and nodded her head.

"He has the feet and the size, yes. I think he will be bigger than you, Pieter," Cilla commented. Lauren smiled back at her husband.

"Stephen," she began, "I like it." Pieter stroked his chin as he continued to think the name through.

"Lauren, I think we should call him Stephen Inham. In the language of my father, Inham means little inlet or stream. He was born here, beside our stream, not half a mile from the inlet we call our harbor. You should see the way he stares at that waterfall. Something tells me he will have a lifelong love of all things wet, be it the ocean or a mountain stream or the mighty Orinoco. You can see it in him already," Pieter added. Lauren laughed with delight.

"Pieter, he has barely been in this world an hour now, and you seem to think you know his entire future already.

He is just a little boy, a baby. His future cannot be mapped out the same way you have done for the seas of the New World, after all. Stephen Inham. It's perfect," Lauren commented.

Cilla nodded in agreement and looked to the heavens. The moon was on high, even though it would be hours before darkness.

"He is a July baby, which makes him a Cancer, ruled by the moon and the element of water." Pieter looked into Lauren's eyes and then rolled his own, if only because he was not facing Cilla. For the moment, the captain would entertain her superstitions.

"Well my dear Cilla," he began. "If that is what you believe, then I say he shall rule all the waters of this world and the moon as well!"

Pieter looked skyward and stretched out his arms in exaggeration while both of the women giggled at his antics. Pieter then slowly knelt down beside his wife, and gently embraced her and his son together.

"My little *Lunar Procer*," he said softly, as he looked over baby Stephen.

Lauren stared back inquisitively. She was forever curious of Pieter's use of foreign languages. He smiled wide and stared kindly back at her.

"It means Prince of the Moon," he added, as he pulled himself onto the lounge chair. Once at her side, Pieter and Lauren lay together for a while with little Stephen. And there, the three of them watched, as the spectacle of a mid day moon slowly crossed the heavens into what would soon be Stephen's first night on earth.

CHAPTER TWO

El Ladrón de Almas

Nearly 450 miles south of Statia, dusk was descending rapidly on the small port town of Nueva Cádiz, a primitive Spanish settlement on the island of Cubagua.

Together, with El Isla de Margarita and Coche Island, this cluster of islands was once a Spanish stronghold, and a gateway from the Caribbean Sea into the South American continent.

It had been nearly a year since the forces of Jeringas Mortifer had overrun the Spanish garrisons and claimed the islands as part of his burgeoning empire. But unlike the slave uprising on Camahogne, there were no acts of decency toward any of the Spanish survivors that inhabited them.

Most of the Spanish men were wiped out in the bloody battle that determined the fate of the island. Spanish women who survived the initial onslaught were kept as the spoils of war. Many of them were forced into the lives of 'comfort girls.' That is, Mortifer's military captains only spared these women so they could rape them at will. Others were brutalized in a variety of horrifying fashions, as a twisted form of entertainment for the soldiers. Some of those imprisoned chose death by their own hand. Others were simply murdered for sport.

The Spaniards' children suffered fates no better. Generally they were sent into the gem mines inland, where small hands and small bodies that could crawl into small places were an asset to the adult diggers.

Any of the captives who managed to survive found themselves enslaved to an occupation of one kind or another. But none of the island's history was of any concern to the shadowy figure who was due to arrive on Cubagua by sundown.

He was someone Jeringas Mortifer personally sent to Nueva Cádiz on that particular evening, to serve a very particular purpose. Few men had ever seen him and lived to describe him. His stature was massive, somewhere around 6 feet 8 inches, maybe taller, and he had huge shoulders, like those of a great bear.

Upon these shoulders, he wore grey metal armor inscribed with the markings of a language that predated all of recorded human history. The armor stretched up around his neck like something of an elongated and upright rigid collar. The collar itself spanned as high as his own cheek bones, and the great helm he wore fit perfectly within it. Together they formed an impenetrable skull and neck protection that still allowed his head to swivel 180 degrees.

At the crown of his helm stood five menacing spires of four inches apiece, with the fifth spire slightly taller, and positioned just above his brow. The very design of this helm only helped exaggerate his already imposing height. At the base of the tallest spire, a seven pointed star made of the purest silver had been inlaid in its center, and it shined as a bright paradox against the charcoal stained metal.

Beneath the massive steel head and shoulder apparatus, he wore a segmented leather brigandine that was oiled and rubbed with spent charcoal so the color would match the steel. If not for the intricate inscriptions that matched those upon the steel, his torso armor might have been mistaken for a hide taken from the underbelly of a massive anaconda.

The base of his brigandine was cut into strips, which gave him the appearance of wearing an armored tunic. His massive thighs were also covered in segmented charcoal leather, much like the design of his brigandine.

Upon his feet he wore heavy armored boots that by themselves, possessed a formidable assortment of weapons. The steel greaves that ran from the top of his foot to the base of his knee had sharpened spikes that became exposed with his leg bent. These he used to impale an unsuspecting opponent with an outward knee thrust. The toe of each boot had a short, sharpened prong. When combined with the incredible reach of his kick, these spikes were devastating in their effectiveness.

He was also a master swordsman, and when participating in large scale battles, he favored the Zweihander, or two handed great sword, a design perfected by the mercenary German Landsknechts. Since he was not nearly as fast as he was strong, he always carried a good length of sturdy rope with a meat hook securely attached to each end. This device he used to capture fleeing opponents. By flailing one end of the rope in a downward stroke, he could pierce the fleet of foot just above the collar bone with the hook, and yank any would be escapees right back into his powerful grasp.

But his general purpose weapon, the one he carried at all times, was a custom made pole arm that was part sword, part spear, and all carnage. It was a sturdy shaft of wood roughly five feet in length with a double edged hewing blade that measured around 30 inches. At the base of the blade were four parrying hooks forged at 90 degrees to one another that were used for equal parts offense and defense.

And, as if to leave no detail out, even the butt cap was a small blade, like an ulu knife, affixed to the bottom of the wooden shaft.

He could throw this pole arm with lethal precision up to thirty yards, dismount a riding warrior from his horse with ease, or swiftly decapitate multiple foes in a melee. In short, he was a brutally efficient killing machine. However, these traits were only the beginning of his value to Jeringas Mortifer.

There was no mistaking his presence when he appeared. When he passed by, anyone standing in his wake could feel the temperature drop by a good forty degrees. The very shadow he cast seemed to suck the light out of any room that he entered. When angered or inspired, his eyes glowed an intense yellow hue beneath his great helm, and one could hardly ever tell which way he was looking. Even the bravest of Mortifer's army captains shivered in his presence.

The king showed he was not entirely bereft of humor by most often referring to him as *Angelis*. The Spaniards called him *El Ladrón de Almas*, or The Thief of Spirits, but to everyone else, he was known more commonly as The Soul Collector.

When the *Unda Jaulaor* pulled into the port of Nueva Cádiz, a small platform was slowly lowered from its starboard side to the wooden docks. The Soul Collector's boots thundered loudly as he crossed the wooden planks toward the assorted small buildings that awaited him upon land. A small squad of six elite soldiers followed just behind him.

In the same instant The Soul Collector's boot touched down on the island of Cubagua, a bolt of lightning flashed brilliantly, followed immediately by a crack of powerful thunder that shook every building right down to its foundation. A stiff wind suddenly kicked in, whipping the Soul Collector's war tattered cape in various directions. He paused briefly on the main road, scanning the buildings until he recognized the stockade.

His squad fanned out, three to each side of the stone lined street, and without saying a word, they all proceeded down the dimly lit road to the jail house. As The Soul Collector stepped onto the covered porch, the two lanterns on either side of the entryway dimmed noticeably, and nearly extinguished altogether.

One of the soldiers stepped up to the door, and banged on it three times with the butt of his crossbow. When the door opened, a man of small stature greeted the archer, and then quickly stepped aside as The Soul Collector ducked down to clear the entryway. The squad of elite soldiers remained on the porch, and guarded the only way in or out.

The jailer was a full eighteen inches shorter than The Soul Collector, and though he had dealings with him in the past, he always found his towering presence unnerving.

"Where are they?" asked The Soul Collector. His voice was deep, dark, and menacing, yet proper sounding. The jailer was a converted Carib mainlander, and knew few words other than his native tongue, but he understood his guest well enough.

He quietly beckoned The Soul Collector to follow him down a corridor where the ceiling hung so low, the larger figure had to bend over considerably to keep pace. The hall then opened into a large room, with two corners segmented into jail cells by iron bars that ran from the floor into the ceiling.

In the left cell stood a man of about twenty years, wearing a Spanish naval uniform, likely that of a petty officer. His face was marked with bruises, his lower lip split, and the white of his right eye was completely red from a broken blood vessel. In the right cell, another man of about thirty years, wearing a similar uniform, was quietly seated. The adornments on his breast were that of a ship's commander. By contrast, his face had barely a mark on it, and he initially seemed uninterested in the jailer's sudden appearance.

The young sailor's eyes widened at the sight of the hulking, iron clad form that galumphed loudly into the room. The commander opposite of him quickly launched to his feet to get a better look, but then slowly retreated to the corner of his cell as he felt the chilly air begin to encircle him. The commander pointed to The Soul Collector as his younger comrade looked to him for guidance.

"El Ladrón de Almas!" the commander blurted. His voice was shaking and fragmented with terror. He was so frightened, he hardly even noticed that his own breath had become visible. The Soul Collector smiled beneath his helm, and though his mouth was not discernible behind the metallic veil, the two Spaniards could almost *feel* him grinning back at them.

"So you know who I am. Good," the towering figure growled. The two men could actually feel his booming voice as it echoed off the stone walls, while the twin kerosene lanterns that hung just outside the hall struggled to remain alight.

"And I know who you are," he continued. "Whether either of you live to see another dawn will depend entirely on what usefulness you provide for me this evening."

The two captives were members of the Spanish Armada, and they previously called Camahogne their home. When the slave rebellion reached its apex, the two men went into hiding. After the fighting subsided, the pair had stolen a small dinghy and fled for safety. But in their haste, they brought no provisions and had no means to guide their way. They quickly got lost at sea, and landed on Cubagua entirely by mistake.

They had hoped to steal a few days' worth of food and water, then leave without being noticed. They nearly pulled it off. After securing a few rations, they made it a few hundred yards from shore before being spotted by one of Mortifer's scouting crafts. The dinghy was too slow to outrun the scouts, and the two Spaniards, completely unarmed, were rather easily taken by force. The young petty officer had to be beaten into submission, while his commander surrendered in a more gentlemanly fashion.

The Soul Collector took notice of the young sailor's face. "I can see you are a fighter." The young sailor grimaced at the comment and began to feel his legs grow numb. The Soul Collector turned his attention back to the Spanish Commander.

"You told my men that you hail from the island of Camahogne. Is this true?" the towering figure demanded. The Spanish officer could do little other than nod nervously in affirmation.

"Then you lived among the slaves for a time. Tell me. What do you know of the stone tablets that were unearthed in the cane fields there?" The Soul Collector's voice had suddenly grown more patient in its demeanor. The Spanish officer shrugged silently, and then looked to his young companion as if to inform him to follow suit. But the young man could no longer bare the cold air that was coiling around him like some invisible lariat.

"We did not come here to make any trouble! We were heading back to Spain, to our real home, when we got lost. I only know what the slaves spoke of. I don't know if any of it is true. Release me from this cage, give me a bite to eat, and I will tell you more." The young man shivered as he spoke, for really, what he desired was a gust of tropic air and a clear shot to the exit.

"Not an unreasonable request," replied The Soul Collector, who wasted no time signaling for the jailer to go and retrieve some food. The Spanish officer looked across the room nervously, for he had no idea what his young shipmate might say or do next. The jailer returned with haste and offered the young sailor a day old corn muffin and a tin of water. The young man engulfed the bread in all of two bites, and then gulped down the water without even taking a breath in between.

When the jailer unlocked the cell door, the young man suddenly leapt forth, and rammed his shoulder into the iron bars. The weight of the door pushed the diminutive jailer back on his heels, and with The Soul Collector positioned in the middle of the room, the opening to the main corridor was unobstructed.

The young Spaniard made a dash for the exit, and quickly disappeared down the hall. The jailer, now thoroughly embarrassed, heaved the wrought iron cell door closed where it smashed loudly back into its frame. He immediately grasped a small, silver flintlock from his holster, and made a motion as if to pursue the young Spaniard, but The Soul Collector waived him off.

At the other end of the hall, they could hear the prisoner's footsteps quickly putting distance from the room, and then the jailhouse door went flying open. The young Spaniard barely made three running steps into the street before he felt the sting of a crossbow bolt pierce the back of his thigh through the hamstring. The petty officer yelled out in pain and then crumpled face first into the cobblestones.

Before long, two of The Soul Collector's elite guards had dragged the wounded Spaniard back down the dim corridor, and deposited him impetuously at The Soul Collector's feet.

Just as the two guards turned their backs and began to depart, the young Spanish sailor grasped the crossbow bolt and jerked it back out of his leg.

Even as blood gushed from the deep and painful wound, the young man leapt toward the back of the archer, with the intention of stabbing him, using the same arrow he had been shot with. But this time, The Soul Collector was ready, and seized the young Spaniard's arm with a grip as powerful as the jaws of a jaguar.

The Soul Collector then ripped the bolt from the young man's grasp, and snapped it like a small twig using only his thumb. With his free hand, the young sailor pounded at The Soul Collector's arm and chest, trying to break free, as the massive gray clad figure chuckled in a lurid amusement.

The Soul Collector briefly released the young man's arm, but then immediately took hold of the sailor's shirt, lifting him more than a foot off the ground with just a single hand. The young Spaniard was suddenly petrified and ceased to struggle. The jailer, sensing exactly what was to come, retreated to the opening of the stockade's main corridor.

"I knew you were a fighter!" The Soul Collector growled loudly. "*I like your spirit.* I think I will add it to my collection," he added in a frigid tone of voice. The Soul Collector then stepped closer to the other cell, as to insure the young man's commander would have no choice but to witness the events to follow.

As The Soul Collector's left hand continued to hold the young Spaniard aloft, he curled his right hand into a fist, as if he was going to punch him right in the jaw.

Instead, he continued to move the young sailor further away from his torso as his right hand uncurled. When The Soul Collector's fist opened half way, a small blue sphere appeared, and seemed to hover just inside of his fingertips. The blue orb then intensified in its brightness, and cast a blinding beam into the young sailor's face.

The young Spaniard cried out in horror, and his eyes widened to a most unnatural state, just as a light blue visage of himself began to escape through his mouth. In this moment, the young Spaniard's tormented eyes were being forced to watch as his very soul was ripped away from his body.

The Soul Collector's free hand seemed to control the movement of the young man's spirit, like he was some macabre marionette operator. The Spanish Commander's eyes never blinked once, and his lower lip hung loosely while the rest of his body remained gripped with terror.

The Soul Collector turned the head of the young man's spirit toward his commander, then back to his own body as it twitched in dying convulsive fits. As The Soul Collector continued tearing the young man's life force away, his physical form began to turn the color of ash.

The young man's hair turned white as his cheeks grew hollow and dark. The color of the young man's eyes rapidly receded into a grayish white solid, rolling backward into his skull, while his skin wrinkled up in loose bunches. It were as though in a matter of seconds, his physical form had aged more than sixty years.

With the young man's soul now completely aloft and detached, The Soul Collector opened his fingers, widening the beam of light cast from the orb. There was a sound, much like a deep breath, that seemed to enclose the room in a temporary vacuum. Then, the petty officer's life force was violently pulled into the bright blue orb, just as the young man's last horrific screams were silenced by an abrupt and eerie finality.

The Spanish Commander could hardly believe his own eyes and was completely oblivious to the stench of hot urine running down the length of his pant legs. The Soul Collector tossed the limp and crippled remains of the petty officer aside as if his corpse was just a clump of dirty towels. The Soul Collector then slowly turned back to the Spanish Commander.

"There is always room for one more," he began. His voice had grown more menacing and impatient. "With that in mind... tell me about the Arawak tomes that the slaves discovered, Commander."

The more senior officer tried desperately to catch his breath, while nodding demonstrably that he would comply with the order. He couldn't tell if he was shaking more from the bitter cold air that surrounded The Soul Collector or the resignation to his fate. The Spanish Commander only knew him by rumor alone. Everything he ever heard told him that *El Ladrón de Almas* rarely, if ever, left any witnesses to his deeds.

"I was a slave owner. But even on a slave plantation, the Africans had their own sense of community, their own sense of order. Most of what I know is from what I overheard or had passed along to me by others. It is not as if the slaves ever saw me or any of my countrymen as friends," he began.

"One day, out in the cane fields, a group of slaves got stuck with a mule drawn plow. It had been raining all morning, and it had rained hard. They were trying to till the soil when the plow just stopped in the mud. They had to take the whole thing apart in order to free the mule. A group of the black men gathered around the place where this incident happened and began to dig out the plow. They uncovered a pair of stone tablets wrapped in some kind of animal hide. And then, as if it were a sign from the heavens, the rain simply stopped. The clouds parted, and the sun shined everywhere, glistening upon the wet land and flora. The slaves began to celebrate, holding the stones over their heads, and dancing. One of the foremen, an

Arawak we employed at the time, went to investigate. He told us the writing on these two tablets was just the gibberish of an old culture. 'Stone men who prayed to stone gods,' he told us. But the next day, our Arawak foreman returned with a shaman..." The Soul Collector stepped forward, and eyed the Spanish officer closely.

"What is the name of this... *shaman*?" The Soul Collector's voice had become a nearly indecipherable growl.

"I don't know. I only heard him referred to as 'Peiman.' I don't know if that is a name or a title," recalled the officer. The Spaniard's voice was rattling, and climbing in pitch.

"Go on!" the hulking figure barked in reply.

"This... Peiman, as he was called, seemed to understand the symbols and markings etched upon the tomes. Every night after dinner, he read from the tablets to the Africans. He usually read from dusk to total darkness. It seemed harmless enough. These tomes, as you called them, were of no value to any of us. And, it seemed that the blacks rather enjoyed the storytelling of this man, Peiman. They hung on his every word as he spoke. Rarely did our slaves go to bed at night so quietly, and so orderly. But that is exactly how they behaved at the conclusion of Peiman's readings. They awoke early every morning, full of energy and vigor, and they worked hard. They were more agreeable to command. But it must have all been for show. These tomes were only twelve by eighteen inches, and only inscribed on one side. I would have thought that, fully translated, they could be read in a matter of minutes. But this Peiman, he came back at dusk every day for about a week. And after the seventh night of his reading, the eighth day after the discovery of the tomes, the slaves rose up against us. They screamed about... destiny... killing their oppressors, and the coming of a child. The 'Child of Prophecy,' they said. And, they said it was this Child of Prophecy that would free all the Caribbean lands of evil. It was all very difficult for me to follow. The Africans spoke a mixture of their own tongue, and ours, and that of the Arawak as well. I did not understand everything I overheard. But I saw many of my countrymen speared to death or cut apart by sickle. The young man over there, the one you... dispatched... he and I barely escaped with our lives."

The Spanish commander felt the foul moisture that clung to his pants beginning to grow cold. Once he caught a whiff of his own scent, and realized what he had done to make his breeches soaking wet, he sat down and began to weep in shame.

The Soul Collector quietly studied the Spaniard's words in detail. He was convinced the commander had been fully forthcoming. Time was now of the essence, and he quickly determined his time henceforth would be better spent in pursuit of the shaman.

"What island did this... Peiman say he came from?" asked The Soul Collector.

"He never told us," replied the Spaniard. The Soul Collector then motioned for the jailer to come and open the commander's cell. When the iron door creaked open, the Spaniard was completely taken aback. For a moment, his spirits lifted, as it appeared that for his honesty, freedom was to be his reward after all.

The Spaniard slowly walked forth, shivering visibly, as he struggled to place one foot in front the other.

"Just... one more thing," The Soul Collector abruptly added.

Once the Spaniard's back was in view, The Soul Collector reached over his shoulder, and removed his wicked pole arm from its sheath. When the Spaniard turned to face him, he felt the cold steel of the Soul Collector's hewing blade pierce right through his abdomen. The Spaniard made a sound much like a whimper while having the wind violently knocked out of him.

"I fathom that you would turn on your king, or better yet, your own father, if it meant saving your skin," said The Soul Collector. His words echoed with a mixture of both compassion and disappointment as he slowly twisted the blade protruding through the Spaniard's midsection. The Spanish Officer grunted aloud in pain, as he vomited blood uncontrollably down his chin.

"You are a coward. *Your spirit...* It does not interest me at all," the towering hulk concluded, in a most cold and collected voice. "Die slowly," he added, and then violently ripped the blade sideways through the officer's stomach.

A mixture of blood and innards poured from the gaping wound, and splattered all about the floor as they landed. The random outline of crimson pools began to form a somber contrast to the perfectly square yellow stones in the floor. The Soul Collector calmly cleaned the blade of his spear, and then returned it to the holster slung over his back.

"Feed their remains to the sharks, both of them," he commanded to the jailer. "And, unless Lord Mortifer himself should be the one to inquire, as far as you know, I... was never here." At the conclusion of his orders, the Soul Collector vanished back into the dark corridor and quickly returned to the street.

The wind larruped fiercely from behind him, just as his squad took up their positions on either side of the road. He could hear metal clinking all around him. Pea sized hail began to fall from the sky, rattling his massive spiked helm rhythmically as his boots thundered down the cobble lined path. When he looked to the sky, he could see no moon, no stars, no light other than the occasional flash of lightning.

And this comforted him, for he and the great expanse of blackness above shared a certain kinship. He felt the powers that be, the dark forces of the continuum, were now watching his every move. In that moment, he felt destiny had led him to the exact place and time he was meant to be.

So begins the events that will forever shape the future of this world. So now, the hunt has begun, he thought. Hidden beneath his imposing steel helm, The Soul Collector's face smiled ever so faintly as he turned toward the dock and made haste back to his vessel.

CHAPTER THREE

CURIOUS VISITORS

Back on the island of Statia, with his wife and newborn child fast asleep, Pieter found himself restless, and decided to take a walk to the pier where his ship was tied down for the night. The wind had been picking up, and his collection of assorted chimes rang peacefully in the crisp evening air as he stepped outside.

At times, the July heat could be unbearable, even at night, which is why he found his lack of slumber on this particular night so confounding. The house felt fresh and the air had been thoroughly cleansed by the breeze. There was none of the stagnant humidity that too often lingered indoors. Rarely did his home feel so comfortable on a mid summer's eve.

Given the angst and excitement both he and his family had been through during the day, sleep should have found him easily. Instead, he found himself wide awake, and inexplicably drawn out to the water's edge.

As he walked across the yard, he could just barely see a dim light flickering through one of the windows of Franklin's house.

Probably just a candle they forgot to blow out, he thought. A couple of small torches near the village square still fluttered across the way. Pieter focused on the wavering light source since most of the area around him bordered on total darkness. As he made his way to the main trail, he could still hear the pleasant ringing of his homemade wind chimes.

Once he reached the pathway that led down to the dock, the chimes faded from his ears, overtaken by the sounds of the rolling sea. Soon, he found himself standing on the pure white sands of his island's shore.

The moon had almost set. Its white radiance glimmered from the far horizon across the water, all the way to the beach beneath his feet. He closed his eyes momentarily and listened to the gentle cadence of breaking waves. He smiled after a time, noting how upon every fourth wave, the *Vissen* gently knocked against the wooden dock it was moored to.

Thunk.... Thunk.... Thunk.... He had probably heard the sound a thousand times before, but he had never found it so pleasantly serene as he did at that late night hour.

Pieter continued his stroll to the end of the dock where he stood motionless for a while. He breathed in deeply through his nose, savoring the scent and the flavor of the warm, salt laden air as it passed over his palate. *This world is truly magnificent,* he quietly reflected.

Way off in the distance, to the south, he could see the irregular flashes of light from a thunderstorm. The wind was also blowing south, so he was not concerned about the storm heading in his direction. Yet, he found his eyes transfixed on the spectacle.

For he knew well enough the proximity of the clouds. Far south, well beyond what his eyes could actually perceive, he knew the coast of Venezuela lay there.

Rarely did he see the skies toward the southern mainland at peace anymore. No, the skies on the southern horizon were ablaze in shades of yellow, orange, and violet, as if the very air was somehow angered, and in the midst of a great battle with the land below.

"It's not heading this way."

The voice from behind instantly startled Pieter so much he nearly leapt into the water.

"Franklin! My god, man, you could have announced yourself sooner you know," said the captain, somewhat angrily.

"I know. But then I wouldn't have seen you nearly jump free from your skin!" Franklin replied, doing his best to avoid breaking into laughter.

"Having a hard time sleeping, Pieter? I never see you out wandering this late." Pieter turned his attention back south to the violent skies.

"Yeah, you could say that," Pieter answered, just as he took a seat on the edge of the dock.

"Anything on your mind?" Franklin asked as he sat down to join him. Together, their four feet swung freely from the dock's edge above the slow rolling waves.

"I suppose there is, but then, I cannot seem to grasp what it might be. The day sort of snuck up on me I guess. It hasn't sunk in totally." Franklin smiled, and nodded knowingly.

"The transition from expecting to being a father can be swift and overwhelming. Here, take a pull from this," said Franklin, as he passed a bottle of dark rum to Pieter.

"Is that the secret?!?" Pieter asked excitedly, as he took the bottle. The taste was both sweet and potent, but thoroughly enjoyable. Franklin laughed in return and shook his head.

"No, I am afraid there isn't any magic potion for what ails you. Your whole life will change now. But it is a good change. Every decision you make will have a new meaning. Fatherhood makes a man focus, and brings clarity into his life. Tonight we drink, and tonight we celebrate." Franklin rose the bottle high in the air before taking a swallow for himself.

"Let's not get in over our heads," said Pieter, as he reached back for his turn at the rum.

"Do you actually think your wife will let you work in the morning?" Franklin inquired with a grin. "If yours won't stop us at the dock, mine will. You are truly mad if you think we have much to worry about tomorrow, Pieter. I pulled the day's catch and strung it in the smokehouse for you. By morning it will be ready for market."

Pieter took another lengthy swig from the bottle, and swished the savory dark rum around the back of his tongue before he swallowed.

"I appreciate that you took care of that for me. Only half a day's catch. We won't fetch much at market, but it will be enough," said Pieter, as he passed the bottle back to his first mate.

Franklin and Pieter both stared in silence at the southern horizon for a bit. Clouds from the north began to drift in overhead, and as the inlet began to gather a chop upon the water, the air grew moist and thick.

"Storm south, storm north. It is going to rain here by sunrise I think," said Pieter, his eyes squinting as he focused on the distant bright flashes.

"It's always storming south. Nothing new about that, Captain. What a dark and miserable place that must be. I have no desire to ever get up close and personal with that dreary land." Franklin shook his head as he stared back at Pieter, and then to the mainland once more.

"No one goes there now. At least none who go ever seem to return. But I have to agree with you, Franklin. I never see the sun shining on the horizon toward the mainland anymore. It wasn't always that way. They say a great fortress lies there, in the middle of a town they call Caracas, not far from the sea. There, and near the town, they say Mortifer's followers number in the thousands. I cannot imagine the appeal of a place that almost never sees the light of day." Franklin nodded as he passed the bottle once again.

"I have wondered the same, many times now. It is hard to distinguish the truth from the exaggerations from the phony legends, given everything we hear these days. He is like a plague. When he conquers some outpost or settlement, nobody ever leaves, nobody ever escapes. The ones that survive seem to stay by their own accord, to live in his service. I fear the day will come when Mortifer desires these islands. I fear one day we will square off in battle against people we once knew. I have seen enough of war, Pieter. I was raised in the midst of war. Be thankful you are a younger man than I. Be thankful you spent your childhood learning words and math and agriculture and books. I know the alternative, much too well in fact."

Pieter studied his more senior friend for a moment. He knew what Franklin had said was true. Though Pieter served in his country's army, he only served the two years mandated by law. Pieter was experienced in handling weapons, and was quite skilled with them in his own right.

But Franklin, he experienced hand to hand combat, claimed lives under the orders of his superiors, and in defense of his homeland. Franklin had seen the horrors of war up close. He had lived it. Pieter knew there was a stark difference between living in war and merely reading about it.

"I do not believe Mortifer will come this way. He has already angered the Spanish monarchy by his actions on the mainland south and the islands nearby. He has taken too many of their outposts, murdered too many of their soldiers. I cannot envision he would challenge the Brits or any other well organized power too. He has to know where this will lead him. He has taken some very valuable property from Spain. At some point, they are going to want it back," Pieter said thoughtfully.

"I am sure you are right, my friend. But when? Right now the Brits and the Spaniards and the French are all racing to stake claims to the lands of the North. As long as they are more concerned with beating each other, Mortifer will remain no more than a secondary matter to them. What we really need is for Mortifer to attack a German outpost, and be so sloppy as to leave some survivors. Yeah... let him piss off the Huns!" As Franklin yelled, Pieter's laughter nearly forced him to spit out his last drink from the bottle.

Pieter could feel the sway of the alcohol beginning to take hold, and given Franklin's suddenly animated demeanor, it would seem his first mate was on the same path.

"Yeah, that would do it," said Pieter, nodding in laughter.

"Could you see it, Pieter? Five thousand Landsknechts showing up on Mortifer's front lawn. Wearing those bright colored, pompous leggings, and armed to the teeth. Then Mortifer, looking down from his fortress, knowing a bunch of primitives with wooden spears and rock tipped arrows are the only thing standing between him and an army of men more maniacal than himself. *Now that would be something."* Franklin laughed as he set down the newly emptied bottle of rum.

Both Pieter and Franklin carried on for a while, laughing back and forth at commentary that wouldn't normally be all that entertaining without the added stimulus that only hard alcohol can provide.

Franklin, perhaps sensing that he and his captain were both bordering on a drunken stupor, suddenly shoved Pieter off the dock. Franklin then dove in only a moment after. When Pieter emerged, he found himself laughing even louder.

"You prick!" he shouted. "I don't know if I have any dry clothes that are fit for sleeping," Pieter added, just as he splashed a wave's worth of water at Franklin's head.

"Sleep in nothing but your skin then, you fool!" Franklin returned through his own slurry giggles. "This soon after giving birth, your wife will love waking to that, Captain."

Franklin then disappeared beneath the water. Pieter pushed the length of his hair backward, away from his eyes, and began to backstroke lazily among the fading remnants of moonlight dancing upon the water. He had paid no mind at all to where Franklin went. That is, until he heard Franklin's pounding footsteps as they charged down the length of the dock.

When Franklin leapt from the wooden planks, he curled his limbs inward, cannonball style, and landed but a few feet from where Pieter was swimming. The resulting wave nearly washed Pieter out to sea.

As Franklin turned on his back and lazily swam towards shore, Pieter dove to the shallow sea floor. He returned with a juvenile stone crab, which he strategically planted on Franklin's exposed chest so it would instinctively pinch the first thing it could find. In this case, that would have been Franklin's nipple.

"Arrrgh! You son of a monkey's ass!" yelled Franklin. He began laughing even harder as he tried to carefully pry the crab's pincher from his flesh.

All of a sudden, and for no particular reason, they were like young boys again, acting as they once did while learning to swim on the banks of the Amstel River. Once they emerged on shore, they both agreed to a boy's truce of no more pranks, and then settled back in their original seats at the foot of the dock.

"Well that was refreshing," said Pieter, as he tried to shake the water from his ears.

"Yeah, for you, maybe. I have a crippled teat!" replied Franklin, who was still chuckling at the absurdity of their behavior.

"It is past midnight now. I think I will dry a little out here and then make for the village. I don't want Lauren to wake, only to find me absent." As Pieter spoke, he felt the rum loosening its grip on his mind.

"She is perfectly safe. Dorothy is up, or at least she was when I left. If the baby won't sleep or some other trouble finds Lauren, you know she will make her way to our house. In any event, there was something else I meant to tell you about earlier," said Franklin, while he swabbed his face with his shirt.

"After you left the dock this afternoon, and I was stringing up our catch for the smokehouse, I saw a peculiar boat circling the harbor. It was no ordinary craft. It was a dug-out, and a brightly painted one at that. She might have run ten yards in length. She bore a small mast and a small white sail. Two rowers were in back, a navigator or the like sat in the middle. Up in the bow, there was a woman seated. Now, I don't want to upset you, but I saw *her*, Pieter."

Captain Thomas squinted his eyes at Franklin, unsure if what he heard was real, or just the lingering affects of drinking too much rum.

"When you say, *her*, who exactly do you mean?" Pieter asked calmly. Franklin stared back silently, hoping his eyes would give away the answer before he would have to speak it.

"No, you don't mean that fortune teller woman, do you?" Pieter asked. Franklin nodded in return. "The Seer of the Sister Islands?" Pieter asked for clarity.

"*Madre de la Tercero Ojo*, she sometimes goes by," Franklin answered.

"*Mother of the Third Eye*. I am impressed," Pieter said sarcastically.

"What the hell was she doing all the way up here? I thought she played her little mind and money tricks down on the island of Aichi?" As Pieter inquired further, he could feel his mild and pleasant drunkenness was beginning to fade.

"I wondered the same thing. And, the dug-out, it was painted red. It had the white markings of a big fish...

58

eating a little fish," said Franklin as he looked around, wishing he had another bottle of rum to break open.

"Cannibals," Pieter said faintly. "You are sure of this? I mean, it seems unlikely they would sail the open sea in a dug-out, at least this far from their home. The eyes can play tricks, Franklin." Captain Thomas looked to his friend's expression for averment, but found none forthcoming.

Pieter looked out across the harbor for a moment, and tried to visualize the strange craft with the even stranger party on board. He knew of the woman that Franklin referred to, at least a little bit. His knowledge was based partly on fact but the rest was merely rumor.

The sister islands, as they were known, were a pair of islands claimed by French authority, roughly 120 miles south of Statia. Grande Terre was the slightly smaller island. It was mostly flat and fertile, well developed, and populated by French settlers. It lay to the east of its larger sister island, Basse-Terre. The Sel Riviere, or Salt River, separated the two sister islands. It was well guarded on its eastern bank, and for good reason.

Basse-Terre was inhabited entirely by tribes of Carib islanders. They were all superb fighting tribes, well organized, and well trained. After retreating west from the advancing French Settlers, they chose to make Basse-Terre their last stand.

Basse-Terre was mountainous, rocky, difficult to traverse, but ideal for the Caribs to dig in and defend. The French knew that in order to remove the Caribs, they would need a massive invasion force, one that at the time, they were simply unwilling to commit. The Caribs of

Basse-Terre also had a reputation for killing any would be settlers on sight, and then eating their mortal remains. It was also said that this tribe believed they consumed the strength of their opponents in this manner.

The Seer of the Sister islands, as she was more commonly referred to, lived among the Caribs of Basse-Terre, at least part of the time.

It was widely accepted that she was born to a Spanish mother on the island of Aichi, what is today known as Marie-Galante, some 20 miles southeast of the sister islands. Her father was something of a mystery. Given her age, somewhere in the neighborhood of thirty-five, her forbearer could have been Arawak, Carib, Spanish, or even French, for they all inhabited Aichi at the time of her birth.

She claimed Aichi as her primary home, and it was among the most well developed of the island settlements. It too was governed by French authority, largely populated by a mixture of French and Spanish settlers, and featured a sizable French military outpost. A few remnants of Arawak natives also remained on Aichi, the vast majority of which were land owners.

She was something of a celebrity on the islands of Aichi and Grande Terre. In addition to Spanish, French, and English, she spoke many dialects of the tribal tongues. Men and women from every corner of the Caribbean would travel to her sacellum on Aichi, to hear her readings of the future.

She was supposedly quite accurate in her predictions. Few who received their reading from her ever became a skeptic later. Pieter had seen her in passing from time to time. He recalled that she was rather striking in her appearance.

She was tall for a woman. Her build was athletic, small waist, small chest, with a strong and, more pronounced backside that didn't seem at all out of balance with her frame.

He recalled that her hair was long, it hung down well past the tops of her shoulders, and for the most part was dark brown except for a few notable strands from her widow's peak that had turned perfectly white. Her eyes were large and well spaced, dark brown in color, and her well manicured eyebrows quite pronounced. Her nose was perfectly straight, neither petite nor conspicuous, and her lips pleasantly full.

Most men considered her quite beautiful, in an exotic and yet, understated sort of way. For she never wore makeup, she had no piercings, her choice in jewelry was restricted to a few bracelets made of shells and small primitive beads. For the most part, she wore a simple tan dress, one woven of cloth upon a back strap loom, typical of Arawak design.

The Seer's clientele included noblemen and common laborers alike. New settlers often sought her services before choosing a place to call their home. Sailors and traders often made it a point to see her before returning to Europe, even if it meant traveling a great distance out of their way. Franklin's wife, Dorothy, was among her most loyal and believing customers.

Pieter was a true skeptic. In the case of Dorothy, he attributed The Seer's most accurate readings to blind luck and simple coincidence. Pieter felt that women were more vulnerable to The Seer's persuasions, and he put forth an honest effort to keep his wife separated from her. In fact, Pieter forbade Lauren from ever seeking out The Seer's services.

"What was she doing, do you suppose?" Pieter inquired after a lengthy silence. Franklin returned a look that was hollow and blank.

"I really couldn't tell you, Captain. I am not even sure if she recognized me. I had the distinct impression she was looking for something on our island. The dug-out swung closely to shore a couple of times. But then, it would just loop back around to the far side of the harbor. There must have been a dozen places to beach a craft like that. It looked like they *wanted* to land, but just couldn't make up their mind. So I stayed on the dock and watched. They just circled around. I watched them for half an hour or so. Then I took the day's catch to the smokehouse. By the time I returned, I could see the little white mast growing small against the sky. They were headed back south." Pieter stood up and stretched his legs, while his eyes scanned the shoreline in both directions.

"Do you think they landed at all?" Pieter inquired. Franklin shook his head dismissively.

"I am just wondering if they were waiting for you to leave the dock. Maybe they did not like being watched. I am wondering if one of them, *her* in particular, did not make the jump to land while your back was turned," said Pieter, as his fingers scratched against the stubble on his chin.

"No way. If she had landed, I would have known by now. *Trust me*," quipped Franklin. Pieter smiled and nodded in return.

"Yeah, I suppose you would be the *second* one in your home to know. Huh. It is most curious, but then, I really do think that woman is a lunatic. I mean, she would have to be. The very thought of sailing that far in a damned dug-out more or less proves it," Pieter offered. Franklin then stood up, and nearly every joint in his body crackled in unison.

"That is one way to prove it. The other thing is, look at the company she keeps, Pieter. I have no quarrel with most of the natives in these parts. Most of them are simple, peaceful people, and some are good traders. But the Caribs of Basse-Terre? The cannibals? I pray that Dorothy is never invited out that way for dinner." On that remark, both men erupted in laughter and began making their way back to the trail.

Once he returned to the comfort of his home, barely a moment after discreetly closing the door, Pieter heard the sounds of light rain beginning to fall outside. Then he quietly changed into some dry shorts, and slipped into bed.

Baby Stephen was as quiet as could be in his bedside crib. Lauren had fallen into a sleep so deep, she was nearly comatose. Pieter took some small satisfaction in knowing that he had not disturbed either of them, and gently pulled the sheets up to his chin.

He still had the vision of The Seer, sitting in a long, narrow, brightly colored dug-out, sailing in endless circles about the bay. But before long, even The Seer in his mind had drifted out of view, as he himself drifted into a deep and comforting sleep.

While he dreamt, the memory of the day seemed to go in reverse, and he found himself back in the courtyard, just after the birth of his son. And there, within his dream, he was back laying upon the tumbona where earlier he held his love, his wife, his Lauren, the same way he held her as they lay sleeping in their bed.

CHAPTER FOUR

THE DESTINED PATH

The next morning when Pieter awoke, he found himself alone in bed. The slant of the sunlight that poured in through the windows told him the morning had surpassed nine o'clock. *Damn that rum,* he thought, as he swung his legs out over the side of the bed.

He wasn't particularly groggy, and he wasn't hung over either. He had simply slept way past his normal rising time. If it were any other day, Lauren might have woken him, for Pieter was generally awake and moving about by first light.

Franklin was right. He thought to himself. *There was never any chance I would get out and chase the schools today.*

When he stretched his arms out to the ceiling, and stood up on his toes, his knees and ankles popped loudly. But it wasn't painful at all. In fact, it was the kind of joint expansion that he found quite pleasing in its relief. Pieter felt a little bit taller, a little bit looser, and he was unusually well rested. Rarely did his life and work allow him the luxury of sleeping some nine hours in a single night.

The main bedroom was in the rear of the house, as was the loft that would ultimately belong to little Stephen. The rest of the house was more or less one great room. On the left hand side was something of a kitchen, which was really just a collection of shelves and cabinets for storage, and a few flat spaces that served as countertops. To the right was a sitting area that surrounded a fireplace, one that rarely saw use. Immediately to the left of the front door was the dining area.

There was another door beside the main table that led to a covered porch and an outdoor fireplace. This is where Lauren and Pieter conducted most of the cooking, as it made no sense to bring the heat of a fire into their tropical abode. And, it was here that Pieter found his wife and child, sitting at the small wooden table just outside. Dorothy was busy making biscuits in a Dutch oven while little Stephen fed from his mother's breast.

"Good morning, sleepy man," Lauren said cheerfully, and with a look of happiness about her that Pieter rarely saw. He was about to reply when his eyes became glued to a spread that included fresh mango preserves and a heaping pile of cooked bacon. It had probably been more than a month since his breakfast consisted of something other than corn bread and smoked fish. The bounty before him was so rare that it bordered on divinity.

"Good morning, ladies," Pieter said at last. He sat down and took a single strip of the thick, crispy meat and bit off a little piece into his mouth. He savored the sweet and salty taste for a good while before swallowing.

"Now don't you be spry, there Pieter. Wait for Franklin to join us. You weren't the only one sleeping off that bottle of rum, you know," said Dorothy, though her back was facing him the entire time.

For a moment, Pieter looked like the child with his hand in the cookie jar at the very moment his mother walked in to catch him. He was certain he had gotten away with his drinking affair from the night before.

"Oh, don't be embarrassed, my dear. It's okay that you and Franklin celebrated last night," said Lauren, as she mildly laughed at the expression on her husband's face. Pieter stuffed the remaining piece of bacon into his mouth.

"It went way beyond celebration, my dear. I am afraid I gave Franklin a case of crabs!" Pieter beamed, as he winked at his wife. Dorothy turned around and gave him a look that was equal parts anger and jest.

"I am sure you did. Probably from one of your traps," answered Dorothy, shaking her head.

"Well, maybe not crabs, as in several, perhaps only one. Just ask him how his nipple is doing," Pieter said with a smirk.

"My nipple is fine," growled Franklin, as he dropped a cloth bag of ground coffee onto the table. Franklin looked like a man who stayed up too late drinking.

"Coffee. Bacon. Fresh biscuits and mango spread. Honey, we should have kids more often," said Pieter.

"No, no, you shouldn't. I can't handle the rum like I used to," said Franklin, as he poured some of the fresh ground coffee into a steel press. Dorothy then served up a plate of hot biscuits and filled the coffee press with boiling water.

Pieter cut a biscuit in half and smeared it with two heaping spoonfuls of mango spread. He then folded a piece of bacon in half, and made something of a sandwich out of it before passing the plate to Lauren. He then duplicated the same steps for himself, as they both preferred the peculiar combination of sweet fruit and salty meat.

Baby Stephen was perfectly quiet, content in his feeding. The four of them then took turns knocking off the remains of breakfast, speaking only in small bits between bites.

As far as mornings in July were concerned, this one was particularly beautiful and relaxed. It was the first time in a very long time that the four of them found themselves with nothing to do, or anywhere they absolutely had to go.

When they were all finished eating, Franklin produced a cigarillo from his tobacco pouch and offered one to Pieter. When Pieter saw the offering, he shook his head and waved it off. He had never been big on smoking.

"Well, it would be rude of me to smoke in front of the baby. Pieter, let's go check on the *Vissen*, and see if that fish is ready for market, shall we?" When Pieter looked back at Franklin, he could tell his first mate really just wanted a moment in private.

"Good idea," said Pieter. "I will be back shortly," he added, and then gently kissed Lauren on the cheek. After Franklin lit his cigarillo in the dwindling fire, the two departed and made their way to the waterside.

"I was out here this morning, just so you know," Franklin began, as the two of them reached the dock. "I did not see our curious visitors in the red dug-out. I thought you might be pleased to hear that." Pieter nodded in reply, cupped his hands over his eyes like a visor, and began scanning the open harbor.

"The fish are ready I might add. We turned out a nice, oily batch. It should fetch a good price," Franklin added as he took a drag off his cigarillo.

"Did you tell Dorothy about what you saw yesterday?" asked Pieter. Franklin nearly hacked up a lung at the question.

"Are you kidding me? Hell no!" he replied between coughs. "She would have made quite a stir if I had not given her the news right when I first spotted that woman. And if I did, *El Madre* would probably be a guest in my house right about now. Neither option appealed to me," added Franklin.

"Yeah, I see your point. Come on, let's load up the catch and ready the ship for sail," Pieter said as he turned away from the water.

Between the two of them, they had the ship loaded and fit for sail within a matter of minutes. After briefly stopping back in the village to tell the women of their plans, Pieter and Franklin shoved off and began sailing south.

The wind was not particularly swift on this day, and Pieter knew the pace of their travel would be lazy at best. While he stood at the helm and guided the *Vissen* out to deeper water, Franklin worked the ropes and the canvas to maximize what little wind was present.

"Upon what course are we heading, Captain?" Franklin asked.

"We have a short day remaining. San Kitts is our heading," replied Pieter. Franklin's left eyebrow lifted just slightly.

"Are you trying to avoid running into *Madre de la Tercero Ojo*?" Franklin asked, plainly. Pieter turned around and rolled his eyes at his first mate.

"What do you think we should do? It is a shorter run and the market is just as good as Grande Terre. Look, it's not as if I'm afraid of that woman, and I am not about to go out of my way to avoid her. To my knowledge, she has never hurt anyone. But I get the feeling after yesterday she was not out for a bit of pleasure sailing. I would prefer if she did not waste my time with any of her crackpot fortune telling. Besides, to make Grande Terre and back in a single day required us departing much earlier," Pieter answered with a shrug.

As soon as these words left Pieter's mouth he began to rethink what he had just said. Pieter had to consider that if his first mate saw The Seer of the Sister Islands late in the day before, she might very well be on the island of San Kitts, right where they were headed.

It was roughly 120 miles from Statia to Grande Terre. Even in a boat as relatively quick as the *Vissen*, it was still a six hour trip each way. It was unlikely she managed to return all the way home in a primitive dug-out, unless she and her crew sailed most of the night. Pieter grew slightly uneasy at the thoughts creeping into his mind.

"You remembered to bring the 'buss, didn't you?" asked Pieter. Franklin stepped forward, and opened a storage locker immediately forward of the helm. From inside the locker he retrieved his blunderbuss, a short barreled, primitive form of shotgun, and a matching pair of Dutch naval swords.

Each sword was made of blued steel, and featured a sturdy basket hilt. The handles were constructed of simple slats of wood riveted directly to each sword's tang. Franklin's sword was slightly shorter, a cutlass, with a blade of about 24 inches. Pieter's sword was the longer of the two, and more curved like a saber, with a blade of about 30 inches. Both men, having served in their country's armed forces previously, knew how to wield their blades quite effectively if the need ever presented itself.

As a general rule, they each strapped their chosen sword to a thick leather belt, and Franklin carried the loaded blunderbuss on a strap slung over his shoulder. Piracy was of little concern to either of them. Any pirate who knew how to make a living at raiding ships wasn't about to attack a low value target like the *Vissen*.

However, they occasionally had to contend with a mugger or even a small band of thieves. That was a potential danger at virtually every port among the island colonies. Firearms were rare among commoners, and the guns of the day left much to be desired in the way of accuracy and reliability. But Franklin's blunderbuss was a whole different story.

Both military men and criminals alike knew the blunderbuss was a weapon to be respected and feared. It was basically a small cannon, and absolutely lethal within a range of 25 feet or so. The thick barrel was made of solid brass, which Franklin kept polished to a luster, and featured an intricately carved floral pattern that ran the length of the metal all the way to the sight.

Depending on what it was loaded with, it could take out as many as three assailants at once. The stock was made of maple, stained just slightly, and was rather plain by design. Franklin had only test fired it a couple times so he could become familiar with the recoil and the spread pattern of the shot. Franklin had never needed to use it in defense, which was fine by him. Just the sight of his terrifying weapon was all the deterrent the pair had ever needed when traveling about.

Once Franklin slung the 'buss over his shoulder, Pieter nodded and turned forward to the open sea ahead. The sight of his loyal companion carrying the 'buss went a long way towards putting his mind at ease.

As the sun continued to climb higher in the sky, the Vissen slowly meandered her way around the west coast of San Kitts island.

San Kitts was already a relatively prosperous French colony at the time. The French and British came to an agreement that enabled the Brits to use the port as a docking station for their war ships. British sailors, after all, were good for commerce.

In addition, the British were orderly and polite for the most part. They solved far more problems than they created. The very presence of their uniforms and weaponry made the port far less inviting to those of questionable employment.

As the harbor came closer into view, Pieter could see through his looking glass that several British war ships were anchored close to port. Such a sight was always a good omen, for it meant that he and Franklin might fetch a better price for their catch.

The British had a particular affection for Franklin's secret smoked fish recipe. He used a mixture of fresh herbs and salt, that when combined with the fish's natural oils, made a form of tasty and protein rich meat that remained edible for weeks. This made their catch of great value to sailing men who might not see shore for weeks at a time.

Franklin's vision was so keen, he did not need the aid of a looking glass to see the Saint George crosses proudly on display and blowing in the wind.

"Well, would you look at that!" Franklin shouted. "There must be thirty British masts in port. Makes me wish we had double our payload," Franklin added excitedly.

"Your reputation precedes you, dear Franklin. I think they will smell those fish before we even tie off at dockside, and I thank goodness for that. I was scarcely in the mood to haggle over price with that stingy merchant, Pierre," said Pieter. Franklin laughed at the comment, as he often did whenever Pierre's name was brought up.

Pierre was a short and rotund little Frenchman, mostly bald, with a thin mustache upon his upper lip. He wasn't a bad person, he was just a savvy businessman with a short temper. He also had a way of getting forehand knowledge of the British Navy's comings and goings, a schedule which often determined the value of the *Vissen's* payload. Not that Pierre ever shared that information with Pieter or Franklin.

Once in a while the two fishermen got lucky, and sold their catch directly to the Brits before Pierre even knew the *Vissen* had arrived. This day, as luck would have it, is precisely what was about to occur.

As soon as the *Vissen* pulled into the furthest reaching docks, a young British sailor whom Franklin had dealt with in the past hollered across the water at them. Before long, an officer appeared at his side, and the two men helped tie off the *Vissen* in the shadow of a massive British war vessel.

Pieter was amazed at the sheer bulk of the British ship. She carried three masts and some hundred cannon or more. Pieter guessed her bow spanned a good 40 feet across, with a length of roughly 130 feet or longer. It was, in all probability, the biggest boat he had ever seen. Pieter was so awe struck by the ship, he had no idea that his payload was being sold at dockside for a price that bordered on larceny.

As Franklin counted the coins and filled his leather pouch, he tried to remain calm.

"Pieter! Get to the cargo netting they're lowering. I got something for you!" Franklin yelled.

Pieter looked skyward, and saw two men lowering a wooden crate from atop the massive boat's deck. He barely heard the British captain discussing the strange looking box.

When Pieter grasped the box by its heavy rope handles, he struggled to remain upright and quickly had to set it down. The British officer known as Captain Williamson then walked over, and with the tip of his shiny black boot, he flipped the hinged wooden top open. Pieter bent down and removed a book with a dusty, somewhat worn leather cover and spine. A royal crest of the British monarchy was branded in its center.

"It is an encyclopedia, a complete set, I might add," Captain Williamson began. "It is a little dated, but the pages are all intact and legible. Written in the king's language too. Your first mate tells me you have a young boy, and you wanted to get him some books. There are a couple of nice reference materials in there, with lots of maps and drawings; the kinds of things that seem to fascinate little ones."

Captain Williamson spoke a very proper brand of English. He sounded regal but not arrogant. He came across as a man of power, but one with a great sense of honor and civility.

"I am getting a new set as soon as I return to London," the British captain added.

Captain Williamson spoke of the books as if he were only giving away second hand clothing to the poor. But to Pieter, the bounty placed before him might have taken a year's worth of profit to acquire. Not to mention, for him to acquire a rarity such as professionally bound reading material in their remote homeland was a monumental task in its own right.

"I... I will take them, gladly, kind sir." Pieter stuttered as he spoke. He was unsure if he should shake the British captain's hand or embrace him. Pieter never got the chance to choose.

Captain Williamson sampled the fish and made a face that bordered on pure ecstasy. He then immediately ushered the entire load of fish topside while quickly scaling a rope ladder in pursuit.

"Congratulations on your first son. Take care now!" Captain Williamson yelled from the gunwale. Pieter gently closed the wooden top to the crate and looked up at Franklin with a sense of both joy and amazement.

"Come on, take a handle, let's go below deck and I will show you how we made out!" said Franklin, as he struggled to contain his excitement.

Once below deck and away from prying eyes, Franklin laid a towel across the wooden crate of books and then emptied his coin pouch. Pieter's eyes widened in disbelief.

"That's about a two day's catch worth of gold and silver, on a half day's payload, Franklin." Pieter's mouth curled up into a wide smile as Franklin started to laugh aloud.

"Perhaps I will put you in charge of negotiations permanently, old friend. Franklin, this is amazing! Do you realize that in this crate, we have more books than most men will ever read in a lifetime? By the time I worked up enough money to buy them, my boy might have been too old to teach. It is no wonder the Brits are so smart and can afford such massive ships. Seems all they do is read books."

Both Franklin and Pieter chuckled in the dim light of the cargo hold. Franklin combed out a half day's pay into his coin pouch, and then neatly pushed the rest to his captain. Pieter looked to the coins and then back at his friend.

"No, we split this. We always split our pay, half and half. Besides, you are the one who did all the cleaning, and the seasoning, and the smoking, *and* the packing this time," Pieter stated plainly as he began counting out and dividing the remaining coins. "If anything I should give you a bonus for negotiating so well."

Franklin gently placed his hand over Pieter's and their eyes met. Pieter could see Franklin wasn't going to accept more than a half day's pay for a half day of work. His first mate was just that way when it came to matters of money.

"Your boat. Your nets. Your skill at following the schools," Franklin began. Pieter was about to interrupt but Franklin waived him off.

"Your son was born yesterday. Your lovely wife is at home with him. Buy her something nice and totally unnecessary. I only need to see the blacksmith for Cilla's husband. I have what I need," said Franklin, as he produced a badly rusted sickle with the tip snapped off.

Pieter scooped up the remaining coins and placed them in his own pouch, save for one piece of gold. He then pointed to it.

"Buy Cilla's husband a new sickle. Then buy yourself something totally unnecessary. This good fortune should be shared." Pieter knew it was the most gratuity he could get his first mate to accept.

The two men then piled some empty burlap sacks on the crate of books and made their way topside. It was unlikely anyone would disturb the *Vissen* sitting in the shadow of the massive British warship, if they could even see it from land. Still, Pieter wanted the crate of books hidden just in case.

"It's a new kind of ship from what I hear. The British Captain referred to it as a *First Class Ship of the Line*," said Franklin, as they walked past the wooden monstrosity.

"Sounds fancy," replied Pieter.

"Apparently they travel in groups. First Class ship of the line, Second Class ship of the line, Third Class, and so on. But they don't sail like a pack of wolves. No, they sail in-line, hence the phrase 'ships of the line,' and they line up all those cannons so that when they pass an enemy vessel, they unleash five or six boatloads worth of shelling upon it, all in succession. I think the average French or Spanish Great Ship would collectively shit itself at the very sight of this formation," said Franklin as he poked Pieter in the ribs with his elbow.

Pieter looked back at all the various British boats grouped together, and tried to envision what they would look like in action.

"No doubt. Only the British could come up with a tactic that seems so orderly, almost polite sounding, like people waiting their turn at a banquet. And yet, so cold and bloody effective. I am glad we do what we do for a living.

I am very glad they seem to hold you in such high regard too, Franklin. I would not want to be on the wrong side of these so called line ships," Pieter returned as they walked past the row of hulls.

A tall iron lantern affixed to a large stone base marked the end of the dock. Adjacent to the base was a sun dial set in mortar.

"Meet back here in an hour?" inquired Pieter, as he pointed to the dial.

"Should be plenty enough time for me to get what I need," replied Franklin.

As Franklin made his way up the path towards town, Pieter stayed behind and walked along the shoreline. Once he had scanned over the harbor, and was certain there were no red dug-outs hidden amongst the anchored ships, Pieter moved on into town.

He had absolutely no idea what he was looking for. Having spare money to spend was an alien concept to him. The most wonderful smells poured out of a nearby cafe. In particular, the scent of strong, French coffee filled the air. Under normal circumstances he might sit and enjoy a cup, but the patio was overflowing with British sailors and infantry. So he moved on to a quieter corner of the town's main square to find a jewelry stand he'd seen during one of his visits previously.

He stood there for a while, thumbing through various necklaces until he found one that he thought would appeal to Lauren. It was a simple design of flat rocks in various shades of brown, polished smooth and strung together. The rocks were cut down and polished so thin, they were almost translucent. As he paid the young woman who tended the stand, he just happened to look into a small shop behind the jewelry stand.

He saw her, peering out through a pane of glass. Pieter immediately had the sensation she had been watching his every move since the moment he stepped into town.

The Seer of the Sister Islands had a look about her that was hard to describe. There was nothing menacing or threatening about it. It seemed to Pieter she was just as fascinated by his presence as he was unnerved by hers. Against his better judgment, and against the inner voice that told him to quickly depart and rejoin his first mate, Pieter stepped around the jeweler's stand and headed for the shop. But once he arrived inside, she was no longer at the window. She had vanished.

The shop was just a small textile store, with large spools of colorful cloth suspended by wooden dowels lining the walls. An old Arawak woman sat behind a counter at the rear of the shop, working on a needlepoint flower. She hardly took notice of Pieter entering the room.

"Excuse me. What happened to the woman who was standing here at the window?" asked Pieter. The elderly woman pointed to a doorway behind her. Rows of scallop shells, suspended by lengths of twine, swayed in the opening.

"May I?" asked Pieter, as he pointed to the doorway. The old woman mumbled and nodded in reply. Pieter drew his saber about three inches from the scabbard, just to check the sharpness with his thumb. As he stepped around the counter the old woman took note of the fearsome blade hanging from his belt. For a moment, she stopped working the needlepoint.

"You can bring that with you, but you won't need it," said the old woman. Her voice was matter of fact, and unconcerned. Her English was remarkably good for a native as well.

"Is she alone? Pieter asked before he reached the doorway. The old woman didn't reply.

"Look, I just don't want to go back there if I'm about to get jumped or robbed. I do not wish to find any trouble back there," Pieter continued in an insistent tone. The old woman then reached under the counter and drew a French flintlock pistol that appeared to be loaded and ready to fire. She simply laid the gun on the counter without ever looking back to Pieter.

"I do not let trouble into my store, mister sailor. The only trouble here now is whatever you brought with you." The old woman stopped to look up from her work briefly, then returned the pistol to its hidden hanger underneath the counter.

Pieter sensed he had worn out his welcome in the storefront, and slowly spread the hanging shells to pass into the rear of the building. When he stepped into the next room, there was only one small window in the rear to provide any illumination.

It was basically just a storage room, where more rolls of cloth were stacked. He noticed a strong smell in the air, part smoke, and part fresh cut wood. He bent over and picked up some loose wood shavings from the floor boards.

Cedar wood, he thought to himself as he sniffed them up close, and then continued walking through the room.

An incense burned in its holder on a long workbench set up against the wall behind him. He looked around the room, but didn't see the woman he came to find. As he stepped further into the room, he noticed a narrow exit in the corner that appeared to be the entry of a stairwell leading up. Then he heard the boards above his head creak just slightly. He didn't even notice that there was an upstairs to the building from the outside.

It's not a trap, he convinced himself. Then he headed up the dark and narrow staircase.

Once he reached the top, he could smell more of the same incense burning, and the faint scent of a lit kerosene lantern. When he turned the corner into the room, Pieter found the lantern. It sat upon a small round table, and the only window across the room was completely shaded in thick, black cloth. There were two chairs set across from each other near the table. And the woman he was following, The Seer of the Sister islands, was standing in the corner facing him. She was completely bare naked.

"Oh my!" Pieter exclaimed. "I am terribly sorry, I can come back," he added, as he nearly fell backward into the stairwell.

"That is not necessary. I am not sorry you found me this way. It is what I intended you to see." As The Seer spoke, Pieter instantly found her voice both kind and inviting.

He couldn't help but look up as she stepped more into the light glowing from the center of the room. He had never seen her up close. To look upon her body completely free of cover, he found her beauty intense and commanding.

She was slightly older than he, but her body was youthful and strong. Her smallish breasts pointed upward. Her hips and backside were large for her frame, yet curvaceous and appealing. Even the hair between her legs seemed to grow only in the places where it was supposed to, and nowhere it was not.

As pleasing as it was to look upon her, he was also embarrassed by his unintended arousal. Pieter looked away and held out his left hand, slowly rocking the wedding band upon it with his thumb.

"If you meant to seduce me, I am afraid my heart belongs to another. Please make yourself decent," Pieter implored.

"My dress is on the chair. I left it there for you to inspect it. You will find it has no pockets for me to fill," she replied. With each passing moment, Pieter found himself becoming inexplicably comfortable with the situation. He stepped further into the room, picked up the dress, and held it out for her.

"I'll take your word," he said, and motioned for her to take the dress from his hand.

"That is a good start. I was not trying to seduce you. I wanted you to see you had nothing to fear. There are no weapons here. I wanted you to see how much I already trust you, though we have never formally met. If any other man had entered here, found me as I am, he probably would have taken me, with my permission or not. And you, I find you very handsome. I would have given you permission to have me. But I knew you would be loyal to your wife." As she slid the dress back over her head and chest, Pieter exhaled in relief.

"Is this how you typically reel in new clientele?" Pieter asked sarcastically. The Seer smiled in reply.

"I can count on one hand the number of people who have seen me in that way. They are all women." Pieter could hardly believe what he was hearing.

"Does it surprise you to learn that I am unspoiled by man?" she asked. Pieter stared back at her blankly.

"In one way, not at all," he began, almost laughing to himself. "But in this part of the world, a very pretty and unmarried woman, yes it surprises me. Your suitors must be many, and there are always dangerous men lurking in the shadows. You must be loved and well protected by somebody," Pieter added, shaking his head as he spoke.

"You have a sense of humor to go along with your sense of honor. That too, is good," she said, and smiled warmly at Pieter in return. She found herself having a hard time maintaining eye contact with him, as Pieter repeatedly looked away from her efforts.

"You should not feel ashamed. Think of what you saw as one of those French paintings of bare ladies that dot the marketplace. I feel that if the human form was always meant to be shrouded in secret, we would have been born with feathers. Besides, no one needs to know of this meeting but us," she added, which drew Pieter's eyes back to her own. Pieter inhaled deeply, and nodded back.

"Look, I spent most of the day hoping to avoid you," Pieter said confidently, but almost in disbelief at his own candor.

"I know," she responded, almost immediately.

"I saw you through the window and I just knew you had been watching me. Just like I knew that yesterday you were watching the harbor barely a mile from my home. So I have to know. Why do you follow in my path, and haunt the roads I travel?" The Seer's head swiveled just slightly.

"A strange choice of words," she replied. Pieter stared forward into her eyes without blinking.

"That's not an answer. Why do you suddenly linger about my home, and what is your interest in me?" Pieter asked again, but more politely.

"Do you think your finding me here, today, was an accident?" She returned.

"If you have been studying my movements long enough, then no." Pieter replied, plainly.

"The British captain had some books he was going to donate to charity when he returned home. Did he donate them to your son?" she asked.

Pieter was suddenly taken aback by the query. He felt as if she was toying with him, trying to convert him into one of her followers, or worse yet, a customer.

"I know what you are doing. You could have seen that exchange from shore through a looking glass," said Pieter, as his mind railed against the feeling that was growing within his gut.

"For sure. But I don't have a looking glass. And if I did, it would be a rare tool. I am guessing he gave you the books inside of a box. I have never heard of a looking glass that could see through the wooden sides of a crate, Captain Thomas." Pieter took note of how she addressed him.

"I knew you were going to arrive here today. I knew you were having a child, probably before you did. I knew it would be a boy, before you saw him born. And I knew you wanted books for him. And I agree your son should be taught proper. For I know how special your son really is." Pieter was speechless, even somewhat angry. He was nearly convinced that Franklin or Dorothy or someone had spoken to The Seer, and their meeting was some kind of a set up.

"Do not blame your first mate, he had nothing to do with this. I assure you." Pieter's eyes slowly steadied and then locked onto hers.

How in the hell did she know what I was just thinking? he wondered.

"You are smart enough to know that in my trade, I am never entirely honest. But then, it is not as if most of the settlers who come here are entirely fair to my people. So I have been known to take from them their money, and then use it to buy back the lands swindled from my ancestors. You are the exception to my trade, rather than the rule. I will never ask you for anything. I will give you anything that I can, should you desire it. A whole new world that you have no knowledge of is beginning to open to you. I am here to guide you into it. That is my interest in you, and your family."

Pieter found himself growing just a little lightheaded. He had no desire to be sucked into the world that she was a part of, the one he never believed even existed to begin with.

And yet, there she was, with knowledge she couldn't have bought if she tried, stating his very thoughts aloud as he so desperately tried to keep them hidden. He found himself looking around, looking for something to make small talk of, to change the flow of their conversation. But the plainness of the room betrayed him. So he thought of the room below.

"What's with the shredded cedar all over the floor below, and the smoke?" Pieter asked, while trying to deepen his quick and shallow breaths.

"The cedar repels moths and other pests. The burning sage is to ward off any evil that may try and enter this building," she replied. The Seer then stood up, and slid her chair close to Pieter's. When she sat down, she gently took his hand.

"I know this is difficult for you to grasp right away. Your world will soon forever change, and living in denial will not halt the progress of the many forces at work here. And while some may be evil, know that many of the forces in play are good. As for your son..." Before she could finish her thought, Pieter jerked his hand away from hers.

"That is the third time you have mentioned him. Now, you have my attention, but my heart grows nervous as my patience wears thin. What do you know of him? What are you not telling me? Is he due to be ill? Tell me, Seer. What is it that you *see*?" Pieter's eyes had grown fiery and his voice was filled with urgency.

"He is of good health and shall remain so," she answered kindly. "But that is not to mean he is free of danger. In time, you will learn why he is special, and you will learn it far better from your son than from me. For now, keep him hidden. Tell as few people about his birth as possible. Soon you will know why this is important. For now, I ask that you free your mind from the burden of confusion. So clear your thoughts. Breathe deep and freely. Take my hands. Look directly into my eyes. Just listen to the sounds of the soft breeze outside. Listen to the gulls as they cry in the distant wind. Listen now, carefully now. Hear the sound of my voice, and flickering flame of the lantern..."

As The Seer spoke, Pieter found himself in a nearly hypnotic state, a trance of sorts. His eyes never blinked, yet they were not growing dry at all. She kept repeating the same phrases, from the blowing winds outside to the lantern on the table beside him. Then, deep within her eyes, Pieter began to see the formation of a vision.

As he peered deeper into the black of her dilated pupils, he saw an image, but it was not entirely clear to him at first. He thought he was seeing himself at Lauren's side, just at the moment of his son's birth, but the vantage point would have been from the trees above.

How is this possible? he silently wondered.

Then he saw a flash of light and a cloud form, and when the cloud dissipated, it led to a new image. Within this new image he saw Lauren again, watching over a small child of perhaps three years old. He was building intricate models with carved wooden sticks, of ships and churches and schoolhouses, and as the vision drew closer, the boy looked upward into Pieter's gaze. His eyes were bright and blue, much like Lauren's, and in an instant, the vision delved right into the blue of the boys' eyes and then expanded into the harbor just beside Pieter's home.

Then he saw the *Vissen*, with himself at the helm and Franklin at the stern, apparently teaching a boy of about ten years how to haul the lines and work the rigging. Pieter knew the boy to be his son, and he swelled with pride to see him working with so much skill at such a young age. But then the view swept down upon the deck of the *Vissen,* and as the scene panned sideways, it seemed as if the ship and the sky surrounding it had changed.

Pieter now saw a much larger vessel with three masts, either a galley class or a frigate, he couldn't be sure. The sky had grown grey and cold in appearance. As Pieter inhaled through his nose, he thought he smelled the distinct redolence of burning gunpowder. By the time he heard cannon fire in the background, his suspicion of the scent was confirmed.

As the vision moved forward, to the front of the large brown warship, he saw a young man standing at the bow. The young man was slightly taller than himself, and he wore a heavy breast plate, like one that would belong to a conquistador. A black cape flew behind him in the wind, and it was inscribed with a bright red stitching. Pieter tried to make out the design of the pattern but it was unclear. It was an animal, to be sure, but what kind he did not see.

A pistol was strapped to the young man's belt on one side, and hanging by a chain on the opposite hip was a sword unlike any Pieter had ever seen. Its blade was the strangest shape, a graceful arc, covered in some kind of golden metal like brass, and an ornate hilt of such beauty, Pieter could not find the words to describe it.

He looked deeper into the vision, and he saw war ships, perhaps hundreds of them, fanned out in a battle ahead of the young man, who was keenly observing the action through his looking glass. Then the young man turned, and Pieter saw once again the bright blue eyes.

His face was slightly rounder than his own, the jaw line stronger, and covered in a well groomed beard. Pieter recognized some of the man's features, for he had seen some in the mirror, and some in the face of Lauren's father. He knew again it was his son, more than two decades in the future, and as the ship sailed forward Pieter was stricken with fear. For the vision was fading, but the sounds of cannon fire and destruction grew louder. And then... blackness.

It was like some external force instantly turned on the dark of night, and all was silent. Even The Seer's rhythmic speaking ceased to be audible, and the blackness Pieter looked into had spread out from the center of her eyes.

Pieter began to pull away from her, but the blackness spread until The Seer's eyes were no longer visible at all. They became deep, empty, like a pair of bottomless chasms, and the beauty of her face drained away entirely. The skin beneath the empty, dark sockets seemed so thin he almost could see straight to the bone beneath. Her cheeks became pale and shriveled, her teeth cracked and uneven. The face of the creature before him now was ghastly and hollow, like a banshee.

Pieter roared out in horror, drawing his sword as he launched to his feet and kicked the chair out from behind him.

"Pieter!" The Seer screamed, just as Pieter's backswing reached its apex. Pieter froze. He felt sweat pouring from his temple and forehead. He could hear the sound of it dripping on the floor boards at his feet, and the long blade of his saber shook in a frenzy as he held it aloft.

With just a couple blinks of his eyes, he was right back where he started. He was in the dimly lit room again. The

Seer of the Sister Islands was before him, her face terrified by the blued steel blade which Pieter held above.

"You are some kind of witch!" he barked aloud. The Seer's eyes were beginning to well up as her lower lip trembled.

"What did you see?" she begged of him as she attempted to gather herself.

"I saw through your disguise! I saw the empty blackness behind those eyes, the stare of a foul demon!" Pieter's wild eyes overflowed with accusation.

"Captain, it's just me, you are safe here. I wear no disguise." Pieter lowered the saber, but kept it at the ready behind his back, as he reached forward to touch her face. Pieter gently rubbed her eyebrows, and her cheeks, and he even pulled her lower lip down slightly with his thumb. When he saw her perfectly straight teeth, he slowly backed away.

Pieter then ripped the covering off the window and allowed the light of the sun to temporarily blind them both. He kept his distance, squinting back at The Seer, watching as she did the same. As his eyes adjusted to the light, and he saw that The Seer was still the same attractive woman he had originally met, Pieter slowly slid his saber back into its scabbard.

"I saw visions that I suspect are of the future. I saw visions of myself, and my wife, and my son. A great battle at sea was about to unfold. But then I could only see you, except, it was not you. It was another woman, I think. But she was so old, like she was standing at death's door. And her eyes, it was like they had been torn from their sockets long ago, leaving only hollows of exposed bone and dead flesh. And where the eyes should have been, just an empty blackness. A blackness with no end, deeper than any mineshaft or dried water well."

As Pieter calmed his nerves, The Seer of the Sister Islands listened intently. She examined his every word carefully. Just as Pieter began to feel some relief, a look of worry had overtaken her.

"It has already begun, then. I should have been better prepared. I am so sorry," she added. The Seer suddenly found it difficult to look him in the face.

"What!?!" Pieter exclaimed. "What has already begun? What was the vision I just experienced?" Pieter demanded.

"I saw the same vision you did. I have seen it in my dreams before. And unfortunately, now, so did she. I had no idea she was interfering..." The Seer's voice was trailing away as her eyes wandered around feverishly in thought. Pieter remained still and just stared at her in reply.

"You are correct that the vision was of your son. The future is not yet certain, for the future is ever changing. But this much is clear, we are already being watched. Your son's safety is already in doubt." Pieter found himself growing cold as the sweat from his skin soaked into his clothing.

"Who is watching us? Who is *she*? And of what interest is my son to anyone but my wife and myself?" Pieter asked in a more collected tone.

"I can only guess to some of what you ask. If I am right, *she* is another member of my order, a woman we all presumed was dead. But there were rumors she still lived. Perhaps those rumors are true. Her identity is not important right now, for if the woman I am remembering is alive, she is well beyond our reach."

Pieter slowly walked back to the chair he had kicked over, set it back upon its feet, and slumped down into it.

"She only saw the same visions as you and I. The top of your wife's head, the color of your baby's eyes, these things are all harmless. If she saw your son's appearance as a man, that is useless as of now. For if your son lives to adulthood, it will be too late for her master." Pieter started to rub his temples.

"Her master?" he asked.

"The black king, Mortifer," replied The Seer. Pieter shut his eyes for a moment. He couldn't tell if he was in a dream, or if he really was exchanging preposterous words with a fortune teller in a room above some fabric shop.

The things he had experienced in the moments leading up to this contradicted everything he understood to be real. He was a simple man, living the life of a simple fishing boat captain. He wanted desperately to ignore what he had seen and everything The Seer had told him. She could sense he was already doing his best to distance himself from the events of the day.

"Captain, you asked me earlier what I see in your son's future. I see him becoming an honorable and noble man. I see in him the salvation of the entire Western World. I see the bane of all evil unlike any who has ever before walked this earth. I see the only one who can bring Jeringas Mortifer to his deserved end. I see the Child of Prophecy within his flame blue eyes. As such, all the agents of evil see your son as an enemy, one they will be hell bent on finding. If he is found, he will be destroyed. It matters not, to those in the service of the black king, that your son is just a baby. They see him as a threat that will grow daily, just as your son will grow physically with every sunrise. And they will look for him, each day more determined than the one before. They will seek him, to end his life in its infancy, to deny the world of the destiny your son has been foretold to deliver."

Pieter made a motion with his hand to signal he heard enough, and then slowly rose to his feet. He stared silently outside the window for a time. He watched the activity of the port, how it bustled with commerce, with ships that sailed in, and ships that sailed out. From the upstairs window he could see as far as the path leading to the wooden docks. He checked to see if Franklin was waiting by the tall iron lantern.

His first mate was standing there, with a cigarillo in hand, and smoke billowing above his head. Pieter then looked out beyond, and studied the great British Ships of the Line. He found such comfort in their sight. For they represented the things that were real to him. They represented lawfulness and order.

What power could a simpleton like Mortifer, a primitive witch doctor, hold over a modern military fleet with hundreds of cannon and thousands of trained soldiers? he wondered.

As the thoughts passed in his mind, Pieter half expected The Seer to comment on them. But when he looked back at her, she seemed to be engrossed in her own line of thought, completely unaware that his attention shifted back to his own reality.

"I should be going" he quietly announced, and then turned back to face The Seer.

"I know. The day is growing short and you must return home. I know you are having doubts about the legitimacy of what you learned today. You will seek distance from me and from this meeting. But you can only avoid the destined path for so long. Either you will find it, or it will find you. Then, you will seek my counsel once again. Something happened today that even I could not foretell. I must make myself difficult to find for the time being. But should you need me, you will know where to look, Captain Thomas." The Seer then stood, walked to the window, and repaired the drape that Pieter had torn away.

"It has been... an eye opening experience to meet you," said Pieter. He found himself looking her over once more. He felt he shouldn't care whether he saw her again, but he wanted to reinforce the memory of her visage for reasons he couldn't quite explain.

The Seer then stepped close to him, gently embraced him, and kissed him just barely upon his cheek. She then held his face softly and looked him straight in the eyes.

"The time will come when you will yearn for more knowledge. Questions will enter your mind for which you have no answers. When that time comes, it will be self evident. By then, I will be many miles away, too far for you to blame for things you witness with your own eyes. Then, you will accept what I have shown you thus far to be true. When that time comes, find me, for I will be waiting. Until then..."

The Seer smiled at Pieter, and stepped aside so he could walk past her to the stairwell. He hesitated briefly, and had to fight back the desire to return her kiss as he departed.

Pieter quickly exited down the stairs and back to the store front. The old woman remained seated in the same place, still working away at her needlepoint. As Pieter attempted to walk around the counter, the old woman gently tugged at his arm. When he stopped, she presented him a sack with several yards of new fabric rolled up inside.

"For you, and your wife. Take it," she said. Pieter nodded and graciously accepted the gift, and then left the store in a hurry.

He had already made the decision to keep his meeting with The Seer completely to himself. He saw no value in upsetting Lauren with the events that transpired. He also knew that Franklin might share the experience with Dorothy, which could only serve to complicate things even more. Then, Pieter suddenly realized the strange absurdity regarding his first time meeting this woman.

He had witnessed The Seer completely in the nude, yet she never offered her proper name. Pieter never asked her for it either. He couldn't be sure whether to regret not knowing. As he made some small distance from the shop, he begged himself not to look back. But he was helpless against the impulse to do so.

As he looked up into the second floor window, he saw the drapes were still drawn closed. He took a few steps forward then turned back to the window yet again. And, there she was, smiling cautiously at him through the opening. Pieter smiled with polite subtlety in return. She waved once, and then slowly drew the drapes back to a close.

CHAPTER FIVE

CATIA LA MAR

"I have lost them," she said, with her head rapidly turning from side to side. She was searching, seeking outward, using only her mind. Thunder erupted above the newly constructed fortress at Catia La Mar, and the rain pelting the turret roof was unrelenting. There, in the fortress spire, kept locked high above the coastal plain, sat the old woman who went by the name of Azura.

She once carried the title Mother of the Third Eye, which was the equivalent of the high priestess of her order. Being the leader of her clairvoyant cast, Jeringas Mortifer once made her capture among his highest priorities as he believed that he could harness her power of foresight to aid in his sinister ambitions. Mortifer also believed she already possessed a working knowledge of the lost Arawak prophecy. However, on both counts he was tragically mistaken.

Azura was on Coche Island when Mortifer's forces invaded roughly two years before, back when it was still under Spanish control. While the Spaniards were largely successful in fending off Mortifer's invading forces, she quickly came to realize that it was she, and not the island itself, that was the true target of Mortifer's conquest.

Azura watched in horror as one legion after another of poorly equipped native mainlanders assaulted the island, only to be repelled and slaughtered by Spanish cannon fire and musketeers. In an effort to end the bloodshed, she fled by boat towards the port town of Porlamar on the nearby Isla de Margarita.

She was within sight of her destination when her vessel was overtaken, her companions eliminated, and she was taken prisoner by Mortifer's henchmen. Though her capture was not by her own design, true to her wishes, Mortifer's forces withdrew, and the fighting ceased at least for a time.

When initially brought before Jeringas Mortifer, the king found her to be an unwilling guest and completely defiant to his will. He tried various forms of bribery and offered her many positions of power and prestige within his kingdom. Each of the king's propositions was always better than the one that preceded it. One by one, she rejected all of his advances. So in an attempt to break her, he kept her in solitary imprisonment for most of a year. But she held firmly to the belief that the warriors of her people would eventually find her and free her.

In time, Mortifer ultimately ran out of patience and became enraged by her petulance. One fateful morning he exploded into a wrath of fury. He beat her half to death, an event that left her with jagged and broken teeth. At the peak of his violent fit, he gouged out both of her eyes with a serrated citrus spoon. But Mortifer, even when seemingly out of control, did nothing without understanding the outcome. He knew that by leaving her with only the third eye within her mind, she would have no choice but to use it even more, if she were to see anything at all.

Over time, she began to rely on her gift almost exclusively. She honed her skills and improved her clairvoyance to the point she could spy on the visions of those within the order. Without the sense of physical sight, she abandoned all hope of ever escaping. The longer she remained imprisoned at Catia La Mar, the more twisted and heinous she became. Her anger festered for so long that it spread like an emotional gangrene, eventually overtaking her, so that she transformed into a willing servant of Mortifer's designs.

"I nearly had him. I nearly had his name," she continued. Her raspy voice was seething with such anger that it left her chin covered in spittle. Across the dim and starkly furnished room stood Jeringas Mortifer himself. He was already in a particularly foul mood, for he had traveled the twelve mile road from Caracas to Catia La Mar by horseback in a torrential downpour. He had been summoned there by his servants, and arrived with the expectation that Azura would deliver a breakthrough vision. Now, it appeared the former Mother of the Third Eye would only disappoint him again.

"Tell me you learned something of value, Azura. Our good friend, *Angelis*, is on his way to the citadel. I expect him within the hour. Give me a good reason *not* to divert his destination to here." When Mortifer spoke, his voice was deep and had a distinctive Spanish flair. He rarely felt the need to shout. In fact, his voice was almost always icy cool and collected, even when he was in the midst of committing the most unspeakable acts of violence.

Azura suddenly trembled with fright at the name, *Angelis*. She knew exactly who Mortifer was referring to. She had felt his chilling presence in the same room only once before, but knew in her mind the things he was capable of. She not only knew of The Soul Collector, she also understood the end result of the souls he had taken. No amount of torture leading to even the slowest of deaths frightened her half as much as he. Azura shrieked and scampered into the corner of her tower cell.

"My lord, spare me his company! I cannot aid you as capably with him near, please," she begged.

"Then offer me some aid of some real value before he arrives," he replied, coldly. Azura crept forth from the corner and huddled beneath a tattered blanket. She smelled the air for Mortifer's scent, and when she caught wind of him, she turned her ghastly, eyeless face toward him.

"The Mother of the Third Eye has made a grave error. She was seeking a man, seeking him for days. This was no ordinary meeting, no. This man must be of some importance. For she lent him the sight of the third eye, and showed him the future. I saw a piece of the vision they shared. I saw the mark of the red lion."

Upon hearing these words, Jeringas Mortifer shifted slightly on his feet. Even in his boots, Jeringas Mortifer barely stood six feet tall. He wore a unique crown upon his head that also served as a form of protection. The helm itself was largely constructed of aged brass with a pair of forward pointing, horn shaped spires that protruded from the rear, which gave his head a devilish appearance. The center of the crown above his forehead featured a flattened, disc shaped convexity forged of solid gold. It looked something like a Mayan sundial, but with very different markings. It also featured a sizable, brightly polished, oval shaped emerald, which was meticulously inset in its center.

A ring made of contrasting white gold, with small sharpened points, encircled the crown's upper third like a miniature fence designed to keep prying hands away from the shimmering green jewel in the center. Hanging from the rear of his helm was a flap of thick leather that kept his hair from becoming entangled in the brass chain aventail that protected his neck. Where the sides of Mortifer's helm extended forward to cover his cheeks and jaw line, he suspended a piece of black cloth to form a veil, so his face was almost always shrouded in secrecy. He lined his eyes in wide black borders, in the manner of Egypt's ancient pharaohs. This way, beneath his helm, his eyes were barely visible. Even in direct sunlight, his eyes were often so dark that one couldn't tell if he had any irises at all.

The fact that he went to such lengths to conceal his identity was a stunning contrast to the clangorous nature of his attire. He wore a wine red gambeson beneath a chain mail shirt that could hardly repel a pointed weapon. The chain mail was made of loosely fitted rings that alternated in silver and gold, an assembly that was clearly meant to be more form than function.

His belt was something of a trophy collection, for it was made entirely of European currency. Both gold and silver coins were hammered flat, so their denomination and origin were no longer clear, and then riveted together. The only part of his armor that was truly functional were the brown leather pauldrons that had been handsomely affixed to the mail shirt, and a series of leather tassets that covered his hips and upper thighs. The general fit of this assembly was one that conveyed comfort and prestige.

By the way these fine adornments jingled and rattled as he walked, none could ever accuse him of sneaking up on them. But then, this is just as he preferred. When Jeringas Mortifer challenged any man to a duel, he preferred for them to know that he was coming. As for the function of his armor, he hardly cared at all.

His skill in single combat was so nearly perfected, he was virtually without a defensive weakness. Many had challenged him. None who did ever survived. Eventually the challenges ceased altogether. The practicality of his chain mail was never tested by the contact of an opponent's blade, having never received so much as a single scratch.

"The mark of the red lion, you say?" Mortifer inquired. Azura nodded and loudly chomped her mouth closed in reply, as if mimicking a lion's jaw. Mortifer's eyes squinted back in annoyance.

He had heard bits and pieces of the lost prophecy throughout his long existence. But without the ancient Arawak tomes, and without the original texts, he could rarely tell what was speculative rumor from that which was truly ordained by the powers that be. One phrase, however, was consistent, the five words that Azura had just spoken: *Mark of the red lion.*

"What else?" he asked, as he slowly paced towards a barred window.

"I saw the boy you seek, except he was not a boy, he was a man. He bore the mark on a black cape, and he led a collection of war ships unlike any to have ever sailed these waters. Their cannons rained fire, my lord, smiting all in their path. Ships with black sails burned against the horizon. I can only presume it was a glimpse into the future of the very harbor your eyes now look upon."

Jeringas Mortifer felt a shock of cold in his stomach as he peered out the window to the bay of Catia La Mar. Azura chuckled faintly at the sensation he unwittingly shared.

"Enough of your presumptions!" Mortifer growled. "What I need are facts, of which you are providing very little. Need I remind you, once again, whose ship will be docking here at nightfall?" Azura's laughter abruptly halted.

"My lord... Mortifer. Perhaps you should have the thief of spirits come and take my soul. Perhaps I have outlived my usefulness here. I have learned more about the lost prophecy from you than all of my kin put together. You have only earned my service now because of their cowardice, their betrayal, their abandonment. If only you had the tomes for me to read I... Oh yes, I forgot, you blinded me, so I cannot read. I saw something else that can only help you in your search. I saw a face. I was once quite gifted in the art of sketch. I might draw it, but wait... You blinded me. Pencils are useless to me now. Perhaps you should have pondered these things before unleashing your rage in the form of a jagged old spoon. So let Angelis come and take my soul. Let him banish me to the unspoken lower realms of the nether world. I will take the secrets of my gift there with me, forever out of your reach."

Jeringas Mortifer considered her words very carefully. If she were any other servant, he would slice her belly open, bleed her a short while, and then toss her body to the crocs before her last breath was spent. The longer she remained alive, the more he began to despise her defiant ways. But the more the lost prophecy unfolded before him, the more he needed her conjuror's wisdom. It was an arrangement that he detested, for it was the only one of its kind anywhere within his dominion. Mortifer turned his eyes back towards the open sea and fought back his burning desire to lash out at her.

"You have a point, Azura. Perhaps by now I should trust you. I know you have been locked in here for a long time, with little in the way of comfort. As a token of faith, I offer you bread warm from the oven, fire roasted quetro, and a nice, private bath in fresh hot water."

Azura smiled at Mortifer's proposal, and then sniffed the air again, trying to hone in on where he might have moved to.

"With some of that fine smelling soap you use. And I only want women to assist me. Even in my wretched old shape, your guards cannot be trusted to show any chivalry." Jeringas Mortifer walked over to the old, blind woman and handed her a small bundle of cloth. When Azura opened it, the aroma of fresh cut soap permeated her nasal passages.

"You are not the only one with foresight," Mortifer quipped, as Azura gently pressed the delightful block to her nose. "I will send for the girls to assist you," he added, and then backed away. Azura sighed in satisfaction.

"If the new Mother of the Third Eye is right, and found that which she believes she has found, then the one foretold by my ancestors is here among the islands right now. The boy you seek, the one who bares the mark, is born of parents who are not of this land. He has sandy brown hair and startling blue eyes. He, like his father, is white."

The news struck Mortifer like a hammer to a nail. Of all the bits and pieces he had been able to assemble regarding the lost prophecy, none of them pointed to a foreigner. At first he was in total disbelief. But the more he thought about it, the more he considered it might be true.

"Very good, Azura. I will go and see to our arrangement," he calmly announced, and then swiftly departed the tower cell. As the stairwell spiraled downward to the ground, he quietly pondered the history of the New World.

The men who first came here just a few decades ago had done so in error. That may be why those who knew of the lost prophecy always described it as incomplete. The Child of Prophecy has been forever nameless. The ones who foretold of his coming would not have understood whatever tongue crafted his name. They did not have the words in their language to describe the various peoples of Europe. As far as the ancient Arawak were concerned, they did not exist.

By eliminating the natives from the pool of potential progenitors, Jeringas Mortifer had effectively removed 90% of the Caribbean inhabitants from the field of search. If ultimately correct, Mortifer was keenly aware of both the enormity of the knowledge, but also the myriad of issues that could potentially spawn from the discovery.

The power of his army was based on sheer numbers. His blacksmiths were only beginning to understand the intricacies of metallurgy. As such, the vast majority of the weaponry his army now employed was rather primitive. The few guns and cannon they possessed were the spoils of war, stolen in fact, and typically kept close to home to guard his stronghold at Caracas. He couldn't risk losing them abroad, for they were the templates his new forges hoped to reproduce.

Without a name, Mortifer did not know where to look. A white man could have been Spanish, French, English, German, any number of nationalities. There were scores of

European settlements from the tiny Leeward Antilles in the south to the Windward Islands that fanned out north, all the way to the Greater Antilles that ended in the massive island of Caobana. While the majority of the settlements had only a small military presence, Mortifer knew it would be unwise to unnecessarily provoke retribution from any of the major European powers. Moreover, even if he took over the islands one by one, word of his advancement would escape, as it always did.

If he successfully captured the wrong settlement, and his men went on a reckless baby killing spree, the real parents of the Child of Prophecy might get word and flee back to Europe. This particular scenario troubled Mortifer the most, for it would leave the Child of Prophecy unidentified, take him well beyond Mortifer's reach, and virtually assure the child's rise to adulthood. Worse yet, if the child did flee to the Old World with his family, this left the possibility he might eventually return.

And return with powerful friends, Mortifer thought to himself.

When he reached the main lower level of the fortress, Mortifer left instructions to make good on his arrangement with Azura, and returned to his riding company outside. Against the steamy air, the rain felt cool as it pelted through his flowing cape to the gambeson beneath. He took a quick scan of the harbor below.

Though there was no sight of the *Unda Jaulaor or* The Soul Collector, Mortifer was pleased by what he saw. Man made rock jetties spanned into the harbor some thousand feet or more. Connected to these jetties were the floating wooden docks he designed to rise and fall with the tides.

New gun ships, not yet equipped with cannon, lined the mooring slips in between. New hulls dotted the shore line in various stages of completion, from skeletal looking frames to finished boats missing little more than their masts, all awaiting fresh shipments of lumber to finalize them. While these boats might not have had the awe inspiring presence of the European great ships, Mortifer was duly proud of the navy he was creating.

For his fleet would be predicated on speed, a flotilla of predators, and legion upon legion of ocean going warriors were being trained every day in hit and run naval tactics. They were becoming the masters of guerilla warfare by sea.

Overlooking the harbor, about every fifty yards or so, stone turrets equipped with cannon had been erected. They were always manned, ready to fire from on high down to any trespassing ship that dared to come within range.

With one final scan of the harbor, Jeringas Mortifer quickly turned back to his riding company and mounted his shiny black steed.

The Seventh Day of Mirrors approaches, he thought, while looking high into the night sky where the moon was hidden by a thick patch of clouds. *My favorite company of women awaits me then.* Jeringas Mortifer smiled at the knowledge of what was to come.

Then he slowly turned his horse northbound on the twelve mile road to Caracas. Flanked by fifty of his best riders, the entire company slowly gathered speed, and headed toward the towering collection of flickering lights in the distance.

CHAPTER SIX

DAY OF MIRRORS

The twelve mile road to Caracas wound around a sharp bend in between the base of two mountains. From there, it climbed steadily upward to an imposing iron gate suspended between two huge stone campaniles. On each side of the gate, a stone wall some ten feet thick and fifty feet tall made the gateway the only passage through to the city for a hundred miles in either direction.

High above, soldiers armed with crossbows walked along the parapet, ever vigilant of the entryway to the towering acropolis in the distance. As Mortifer's riding company approached, one of his bodyguards whipped his stallion into a full sprint, so he could reach the gate in advance, identify his company, and enable the king to pass without ever breaking stride. Once he completed this task, the rider pulled his horse aside, and the heavy iron doors groaned outward. The promenade of some two hundred hooves striking down on the cobblestone road bordered on deafening. Their echoes carried everywhere throughout the dim valley ahead.

The glowing lights of strategically placed watch towers danced along the mountainsides above. In the sheer darkness, they gave the impression of being suspended magically in thin air. As the company passed between the two mountains, the land opened up once again to green and level fields.

A huge, circular formation of torches suddenly came into view, spilling yellow light into the fields and roadway in abundance. Stone masons worked through the night in an effort to finish a large amphitheatre on the inside of a naturally formed crag basin. Once it was completed, Mortifer planned to host games of armed combat and various contests between men and beasts, much like the ancient Romans once did on the other side of the world.

Throughout the valley, hundreds of simple huts were still visible in the darkness. Some of their windows glowed faintly from burning candles that suddenly went dark as Mortifer's company passed by. And this pleased the black king, because it seemed in a way that his subjects both awaited his return and yet feared it all the same. But his crown jewel, the creation that pleased him most, was the colossal fortress they approached, the place Mortifer called home.

The main structure was massive, stretching into the sky well over a hundred feet at the tallest spires. The entire exterior was made of blue granite, a rare and extremely heavy stone that only occurred hundreds of miles away in the coastal region of modern day Brazil.

It had taken Mortifer nearly forty years to complete it. Hundreds, if not thousands of men and livestock perished during the process of collecting, cutting, relocating, polishing, and assembling these stones.

During an uncommon day of solid sunshine, Mortifer's fortress glowed an eerie light blue color against the greenery that surrounded it. While during a day of overcast and clouds, the color of the stones darkened, and it gave off the distinct impression that it was freezing cold.

The road made one final, but gradual ascension upward, and the entire company slowed their advance. Mortifer's men always crossed the moat with care. The water beneath was deep, foul smelling, and teeming with crocodiles that grew close to twenty feet in length. The crocs were often attracted by noise and movement, and any man who ventured too close to the edge risked being snapped up and dragged into the water below. The sound of trotting hooves suddenly amplified as the riding company crossed the heavy wooden draw bridge to the main gate on the first level.

Up above, huge torches cast impressive halos of light through the dozens of meticulously crafted archways. Each level of the fortress rising upward was slightly smaller than the one below, which gave the base a pyramid-like appearance. After six levels, the roof line split into two large, central towers connected by a pair of great rooms in the middle. There were about a dozen smaller turrets and steeples that seemed to spring out here and there with no apparent rhyme or reason. But every window, every arch, every last nook carved in the granite bastions served a specific purpose.

No army could advance on the city from any direction without detection from a lookout. The tallest turrets and spires had a compliment of small arms and Spanish sakers; mid sized cannon seized from defeated war vessels. By elevating their firing position, Mortifer gave the sakers an effective range of nearly two miles, roughly twice their maximum range at sea level.

Even if an attacking force somehow managed to get close enough, the dense granite walls were thick enough to thwart repeated cannon fire. By all accounts, Mortifer's grand citadel was impregnable. From a distance, when viewing the fortress against the horizon, there was a sparing resemblance between the gigantic structure and the outline of the king's elaborate crown.

By the time Mortifer passed through the main lower level entrance, the rain had slowed to a light drizzle. He was always the first rider to dismount, and when he handed the reigns of his black horse to one of his servants, he walked back to the edge of the drawbridge and peered into the water below.

The distinct golden shine of reptilian eyes slowly glided just above the surface, staring back at him. It seemed as if the crocs were drawn to him, and on occasion, Mortifer would have his butcher slaughter a farm animal of some kind so he could feed them personally. But on this night, he didn't have any meat prepared. He wanted them to remain hungry. Mortifer briefly looked back down the road he had just traveled, and then slowly turned toward the stairs leading up to the main palace.

Inside, every stone was polished to perfection. Every exposed floor glimmered with mirror like qualities. Every room was decorated with furniture, sculptures, paintings, and rugs, that paid tribute to the native cultures of the region but gave the entire building a feeling of morose opulence.

When Jeringas Mortifer reached the ninth floor, he was not surprised to find a group of both women and girls gathered there. He quickly turned the corner and arrived on the tenth floor, a place regarded as off limits to all but his most trusted servants.

The tenth floor was Mortifer's personal place of residence. It was where he kept his clothes, where he had a private bath, where he most often ate, and where he slept at the end of the day.

As midnight approached, so did the Seventh Day of Mirrors, July 7th. Every month had its own Day of Mirrors, from January 1st to December 12th. That is, every time the number of the month equaled the day of the month, Mortifer and a select few of his inner circle participated in the ritual that was about to unfold. After riding the twelve mile road to the coast and back again, the king felt a hot bath was due.

The same two women always aided him during the Day of Mirrors, and they were meticulous in their routine. They took particular care with his helm, chain mail, and belt when removing them and hanging them on their respective stands.

Jeringas Mortifer was not modest in disrobing before women. In fact, he was very much the opposite. Once free of his armor, he hastily pulled his soaking wet clothes off and tossed them aside as he made his way to the polished granite tub.

His frame was rather average, but his musculature was so pronounced in his chest, back, and limbs, he looked like he might have carried every chunk of stone used to build his castle personally. His skin was well tanned, like a field laborer's, and the majority of his upper body was completely covered in a labyrinth of tribal tattoos. His back and chest looked like one continuous piece of art that branched up the back of his neck and then down his upper arms. The design incorporated Celtic looking weaves and knots, symbols of both the Mayan and Incan languages, as well as abstract drawings of gargoyles, snakes, bats, spiders, and scorpions.

The central character in this grand display of emblematic ink was a black panther drawn on his chest in such sharp detail, it could have been carved in black scratchboard with a scalpel. The two women who bathed him knew the king's tattoos so well that, by then, they could actually spot a single speck of dirt anywhere on his skin.

When he slowly slid into the steaming water, one of the girls gently placed a rolled towel under his head so he could lean backward fully and in comfort. On most occasions, Mortifer would demand that the women who cleansed him be naked as well, but never on the Day of Mirrors.

While one stayed behind him and massaged his neck and back, the other moved about the tub running a bar of soap over one appendage at a time. His body was remarkably free of hair, and he could get by for days without the need to shave his face and neck.

Jeringas Mortifer slid himself beneath the water in one final plunge and when he rose, the girls set towels on the steps leading from the tub to the floor. They quickly dried him, assisted him in reapplying his eyeliner, and were then immediately dismissed.

He preferred a moment of solitude before making his grand entrance. Mortifer lightly sprayed himself with some fragrant oils that smelled of sandalwood and citrus. He then went about combing his hair in order to dry it more rapidly. As he stroked the comb downward repeatedly, he leaned forward towards the mirror.

He scanned his face for any visible signs of aging. Then he did so again, and yet again. Then, in a ritualistic manner only rivaled by men of modern militaries, he dressed himself in perfectly wrinkle free breeches and a long, flowing black surcoat spun of the finest cloth. Once he returned his crown and veil to their original places, he took one long, final look in the mirror. The stroke of midnight was fast approaching. He then returned to the ninth floor.

"Good evening, my lord Mortifer," called a familiar voice from across the room. Standing before Jeringas Mortifer was a relatively short and thin man who was clad in a light gray cloak who went by the name of Hadrian. He was half Carib and half Incan, with short cropped hair and a pencil line beard. He wore a gold medallion around his neck with an engraving similar to the panther tattooed on Mortifer's chest. Hadrian was known among the kingdom as the king's high counsel, but his function was more like that of an Ottoman grand vizier.

Hadrian had lived in Europe for a time where he learned much about their various customs and laws. He advised Mortifer on a wide range of topics, beginning with religious practices and extending all the way into military matters. As much as The Soul Collector was the muscle behind Mortifer's dominion, Hadrian acted as its spirit.

"I think you will be most pleased with the offerings I have recruited for this Day of Mirrors, my lord," said Hadrian, as they approached a group of six women with six girls. The pairings were all related as mother and daughter.

"And you are certain that all of the mothers are widowed?" Mortifer asked in a low volume, so as not to make an echo. Hadrian nodded confidently.

The women and the girls bowed as Mortifer stopped to look them over. As Mortifer paced before them, examining their every feature, every last detail, mother and daughter alike, they all smiled lovingly at him in return. They all seemed willing, eager, and hopeful of being chosen.

"I am pleased, Hadrian. Your work here is finished, my friend." Hadrian quietly bowed and swiftly made for the stairwell. Jeringas Mortifer then began to address the women in Spanish.

Hadrian was feeling so pleased with himself, he didn't even notice the towering form standing back in the shadows of the darkened stairwell. Hadrian would have walked right into him if he had not felt the air before him become so instantly chilled. When The Soul Collector's eyes flashed a bright yellow notice, Hadrian felt his heart skip a beat as he suddenly recognized who was standing at the top of the stairs.

"Angelis!" Hadrian exclaimed, in a startled, but low whisper. "You shouldn't be here. You know Lord Mortifer doesn't want to be disturbed during the Day of Mirrors ritual." The Soul Collector quietly looked to his own feet. He was two steps down the flight of stairs and yet he was still taller than Hadrian.

"I am precisely where I am supposed to be," The Soul Collector replied in an unconcerned tone. Even as he tried to keep his voice down, it still echoed down the hall.

"Lord Mortifer is expecting me, counselor. He only needs his privacy once he has made his choice and taken them up to his personal living quarters. Tell me, *high* counsel, how do you live with yourself being guilty of such *low* acts?" The Soul Collector's eyes glowed faintly, but still menacing as he stared down at the king's advisor. Hadrian's mood shifted from uneasy to utter disbelief.

"I am not about to be judged by the one being who has probably slain more children than all the armies in the history of the world," Hadrian scoffed, shaking his head.

"Let us be clear. I have never killed an innocent. I have only acted as an escort for the souls of children called forth to cross over. The continuum of being always decided their fate, not I. But this arrangement of barbarism..." The Soul Collector's eyes shifted to Mortifer and his audience. For a moment, they both stood in silence and listened.

Mortifer's speech was always the same, every month. He spoke of how fate brought all of them together through the death of a husband and father. He spoke of the privilege of being chosen by the *continuum*. He told the mothers to be proud of their daughters. He promised the girls a chance to transcend into the equivalent of the spiritual Shangri-La of the continuum. And as he spoke, both the adult women and their young daughters alike were mesmerized.

They believed his every word, gripped every promise he made even tighter in their hearts, and felt a sense of love toward their king that rivaled that of their lost husbands and fathers. In some ways, their enchantment with him actually exceeded what they felt toward their departed loved ones. To them, in the culture that Mortifer himself had perpetuated, there was no greater honor than being in the king's presence on the Day of Mirrors. They actually *yearned* to be chosen.

The Soul Collector wouldn't have taken issue with any of this, assuming one word of it was true. Knowing the real fate of the young girls left him in a state that drifted somewhere between disgusted and disturbed.

"It is blasphemy to challenge it. You know that he needs this to survive, Angelis. To suggest otherwise would be a direct remonstrance of his divinity. He is a god, and he is our king. You made an arrangement with powers greater than yourself in order to be here now. I suggest you remember that, lest Lord Mortifer question where your loyalties reside." The burning yellow rings within the Soul Collector's helm slowly faded to a pair of faint glowing orbs that smoldered of words better left unspoken.

Hadrian then began to shiver, as he felt the temperature around him drop even further.

"I do envy you, Angelis. I envy you and admire you. Because you have been summoned to serve him until his destiny is fulfilled. I, on the contrary, only have this one lifetime to be in his service. Pity me." Hadrian then quickly departed down the steps and out of The Soul Collector's view.

As polite and complimentary as Hadrian may have sounded, The Soul Collector knew it was little more than a parting barb. If anything, The Soul Collector envied Hadrian's mortality, and they both knew it.

It wasn't that The Soul Collector was opposed to death if it served some greater purpose of the continuum. To many, he was the angel of death, and he had participated in the cessation of so many lives it would be fruitless to try and place a number on the total.

He wasn't entirely against torture either, and had in fact found it useful at times. He simply couldn't find any logic to Mortifer's rituals on the Day of Mirrors. Moreover, he knew precisely what awaited the chosen daughter in a secret chamber located on the tenth floor.

The Soul Collector was keenly aware that Mortifer could acquire what he needed in a more surgical and expedient fashion. So he was confounded by his master's methodology. But if Mortifer truly was as old as some claimed, a mystery that even The Soul Collector couldn't solve for certain, then the Day of Mirrors occurred twelve times a year for more than two millennia. That would have made the total rituals number around twenty thousand, perhaps even more, depending on when the king's unusual need actually began.

If the dark powers of the continuum saw fit to allow Mortifer to repeat the ritual so often, and The Soul Collector served them both, he felt he was in no position to challenge or question the validity of his master's custom.

While he waited for Mortifer to make his selection, he pondered whether the dark powers of the continuum would ever end their support of the black king. If that support suddenly ceased, The Soul Collector wondered if he, of all beings, would be the one sent to end Mortifer's time on Earth. He found the prospective irony morbidly humorous in its own way.

And if I should claim him, who should then come and claim me for all that I have done in his name? He shook his head and returned his focus to the task ahead.

Applause erupted from the far end of the room as Mortifer made his choice. The black king bid his farewells to the women he was sending home, and then led the mother and daughter of his choosing to the far stairwell.

Jeringas Mortifer, perhaps sensing The Soul Collector's arrival, did not follow them up.

Unlike most everyone else, Mortifer could not feel the chill that came with his shadowy servant. Mortifer could, however, notice when the candles and lanterns suddenly dimmed because his chief lieutenant drew near. But Mortifer's connection to him was far more infernal than that. He turned away at the foot of the stairs and returned to the great room as The Soul Collector's heavy boots reverberated across the floor.

"Angelis!" Mortifer called. "I knew you would make it in time. Tell me what you have learned during your travels." The Soul Collector nodded a brief bow to his king, and then pulled two high backed chairs close to one another. Once Mortifer was seated, the towering dark figure took the seat across from him.

"I have learned much, so let me get right to it. A pair of tomes from the lost prophecy have been found. I cannot say for certain, but I have a strong reason to suspect there may be more." Even as The Soul Collector tried to keep his voice low, his words still echoed coldly off the polished walls and ceiling.

"What makes you think there are more than two?" Mortifer inquired.

"A Spanish officer we captured. He witnessed the unearthing of the tomes. He also witnessed an Arawak shaman who could read them - fluently. And this shaman allegedly read the tomes to a large company of Africans. This, as it seems, was the driving force behind the recent slave uprisings. It seems the shaman knew far more than what two tomes could possibly contain. So the language is not entirely dead. They called this witch doctor 'Peiman.' The tomes were discovered on the isle of Camahogne. It is doubtful they remain there now. I believe this man, Peiman, is still in possession of them. With your permission, Lord Mortifer, I will track him down." Jeringas Mortifer smiled wide and nodded in approval.

"We would be most fortunate to find both the tablets and the one person who can fully translate them in the same place. I have to believe this shaman is smarter than that. He has probably hidden them somewhere else by now," Mortifer said thoughtfully.

"Finding the shaman will suffice, my lord. After all, he has already read the tomes. If there are others, he will undoubtedly know of them and possibly their location. As you know, I have had little difficulty in... *persuading* these tribal witch doctors to assist us in the past." Jeringas Mortifer's eyes shifted from the floor to the hulking figure seated next to him. The black king then burst into a maniacal laughter.

"Yes, *Angelis*, I should say your powers of persuasion are second to none. It would please me beyond words if you were to capture this man, Peiman. He could become more valuable than Azura, and enable me to be rid of her once and for all." Mortifer studied his lieutenant for a moment to see what, if any, reaction would be forthcoming.

"I would not eliminate her just yet, my lord. Not until we find a suitable replacement. I have heard nothing to make me think Peiman has the gift of the third eye. Even if he does, there are no guarantees he will allow himself to be taken alive, or that he will live to be of any use to you. One thing that is certain, he is a true believer. That alone makes him incredibly dangerous." Mortifer shook his head in disagreement.

"His kind is dying out. The vast majority of all native men now swear their allegiance to me. He cannot summon an army out of the scattered remains of his people," Mortifer rebuffed in a tone of dismissal.

"It is not the natives, but the free people of the islands that should concern us, my lord. Because now, this shaman has made whole legions of true believers out of the former slaves. It began on Camahogne, and now there are rumors that Kairi and Bella Forma have been abandoned by the Spaniards. Camahogne has already established something of a government, and a military presence. It is only a matter of time before Kairi and Bella Forma join them in a triumvirate of sorts. I have also learned that a handful of Europeans have grown sympathetic to their plight. At least one man, a former major in the British army, has gone so far as to move to Camahogne permanently, to train the Africans in modern war. With formal training and proper equipment, you can see how this would pose a number of problems, my lord. It is imperative that we act quickly."

Jeringas Mortifer's concern hung unmistakably on his face.

"How many African men of fighting age are we talking about?" inquired the king.

"Estimates vary, my lord. Ten thousand on Camahogne at the minimum. Kairi was the central slave trading station of the Spanish Empire. It is a massive island. In the years leading to her independence, hundreds of slave ships came and went. There could be up to another twenty thousand men living there. These people, they already fought to claim their freedom once. They will not relinquish it without a resistance greater than any you have ever faced before," The Soul Collector answered plainly.

Mortifer sighed loudly, stood up, and began pacing about the room.

"Leave the slave nations to me. Very soon we will have a navy formidable enough to put a stop to British interference among those islands. The Africans will not pose much of a threat if we deny them the delivery of weapons. Perhaps the tablets are still there on Camahogne. At the least, whomever has them may feel they are secure there for now. I have also learned some new information, Angelis, that may be of value to you. Azura believes the Child of Prophecy has already been born and that he is here, among the islands. She is convinced he is the son of a white man."

The Soul Collector's initial reply was merely a blank stare.

"I cannot say this surprises me, given the very recent settlements by men of the Old World at the exact same time the lost prophecy resurfaced. We must be certain of Azura's claim, Lord Mortifer. I would not put it past her to intentionally mislead us into searching for the wrong boy. She has her own reasons to dislike the white settlers. I would not want to see our forces waging any battles that only serve to fulfill her desire for vengeance. We have time where the child is concerned. Peiman, on the other hand, cannot be allowed to disappear or become more deeply entrenched with the former slaves. I need to pick up the trail while it is still warm, and before he rallies even more followers to his cause." Mortifer nodded agreeably in return.

"We should act quickly and in stealth. You and your men operate quite well under the cover of darkness. As such, I have thought about a potential alliance you should explore. We have long needed someone who can pass for a white settler, to help us gather information. There is no one currently in our employ or anywhere in our prisons we can trust. So I want you to pay a visit to Isla Mona among the Greater Antilles."

The Soul Collector's eyes dimmed noticeably behind his helm as he thought the instruction over.

"Isla Mona? My lord, I am afraid I don't understand what alliance we can gain there. As far as I know, no one lives there."

"In a manner of speaking, you are correct, Angelis. It is true that nobody who is alive resides there presently. However, you may find some Romanian... *outcasts*. A small group of men and women who allegedly fled their home country to escape persecution. I have been told they travel from Isla Mona to Mayaguez on occasion. It seems they... *feed* on the primitives there." Mortifer smiled as the words rolled off his tongue.

"Romanians? You mean vampires. I had only heard some trite gossip regarding their existence. I thought they were something that white men had invented to keep their children indoors at night," said the Soul Collector. His voice was dripping with derision.

"No, my friend Angeles, they are more than folklore. They are more properly known as *strigoi*. They are real.

You will find them in the sea side caves on the southern shore of Isla Mona. They, like your crew, do their best work at night. Though you may have to make some unusual travel arrangements to take one with you." The Soul Collector stared silently in reply.

"In any event, it will take a couple days to reach them from here. Hadrian has assembled some literature for you to study. You will want to read up on these strigoi and learn all that you can about them. Figure out their weaknesses. Determine how and if they can be exploited. As for the terms of any arrangement you make, if they agree to help us, then they can keep their island home," Mortifer added, as he rose back to his feet. The Soul Collector nodded silently.

"And if they refuse?" asked the towering figure.

"Make an example out of one. Then if the rest still refuse, you may dispose of them however you see fit. Seek the Romanians first. Then find the shaman. Take any additional men and whatever provisions you need. And, whatever actions you take, you may do so under my authority in advance. I know you will succeed, Angelis."

The Soul Collector departed from the room even more swiftly and purposefully than when he came. As the sound of his boots dissipated down the stairs, Jeringas Mortifer quietly returned to the tenth floor.

He found the mother and daughter of his choosing both seated on his bed. They were silently holding hands, and both smiled up at him in the warm, subtle glow of a hundred candles burning throughout the room. He did not know their names. He did not ask for them. Just as he did not ask for any of the names of the thousands who had come before them.

Mortifer first approached the daughter. She was pretty, but she couldn't have been a day older than fourteen. Mortifer beckoned her to stand. When she did, he gently began to remove the clothing from her trembling limbs.

"It's okay," he whispered to her. As he stepped back, he gently inspected her body with his hands. He then stripped himself completely naked, and joined them on the bed.

Mortifer particularly enjoyed what followed next. While the young girl watched, her mother performed a variety of physical acts with him. The event was not about sex. Mortifer was incapable of actual reproduction. He could be aroused, perform in the typical sense, and even achieve an intense and pleasurable climax. But when he did, it was the reproductive equivalent of a dry cough.

For him, he enjoyed making the elder of the two women love him for the night. And love him, they always did, in a way that was deeply emotional and spiritual. He enjoyed watching a young girl lose her inhibitions by witnessing her own mother in action. He loved building up the young girl's trust, for it was part of the crescendo at the very heart of the Day of Mirrors rite.

Mortifer did have one unusual ability to support his bizarre sexual appetite. He did not need any down time in between his sensual climaxes, and he often needed four or five of them to achieve total satisfaction. He typically looked to achieve several with the mother before he dismissed her. It was a way of numbing himself, so that later on, he could achieve his own rapture at the expense of the chosen.

On this night, as often was the case, the girl's mother sought reassurance from the king before she was due to depart.

"You promise, you won't hurt her?" the woman asked, as her voice labored in pleasure.

"Not at all. She must remain pure to make the journey. I will not take that purity from her. She will only feel the gentlest touching, I swear it." As he replied, his voice seemed honest yet hungry. He would demonstrate this for the girl's mother just once, using nothing more than his tongue on the young girl's neck in a gentle and reserved fashion.

The last passage the three took together. The roles of the mother and daughter were reversed, for now the mother watched as Mortifer gently touched her daughter. When the young girl finally peaked, in her manner of doing so, Mortifer left her body alone, to totter in nervous excitement. When the moment had passed, both the girl and her mother just laughed hysterically at one another, while Mortifer smiled proudly.

As far as either of them knew, this was to be the end of their physical play altogether. Because Mortifer made it clear from the beginning, the girl's virginity had to remain intact for her to 'transcend.' He had both of them convinced he would never trespass upon her in such a way that would compromise the girl's purity.

"He is a god, isn't he?" the young girl inquired of her mother.

"Yes he is. He is a god and the greatest of all kings," the mother answered.

"And now, she has achieved *el cima* unspoiled by man. It is time for her transcension," the king merrily announced. Mortifer then wasted no time in gathering the mother's clothing for her.

Considering they both knew this was to be the last time they would ever see one another, it was hardly an emotional departure. In fact, both the mother and her daughter seemed downright capricious in their collective disposition. As Mortifer politely ushered the girl's mother downstairs, she only asked him one final question.

"When she transcends above, do you think she will see her father again?" Mortifer nodded ever so slightly, as a slippery grin grew beneath his widening eyes.

"She will. In fact, I am certain of it." There was a barely noticeable tone of sarcasm in his reply.

The woman smiled at him and scampered to the stairwell across the great room. She blew him one quick kiss and then disappeared down the stairs. Mortifer grinned coldly at her exit. He waited at the stairs for a few minutes. Once he was certain the girl's mother did not have any last minute change of heart, he rejoined the young damsel upstairs.

The girl was still laying in the middle of his bed, exactly as he had left her. She smiled in fascination and yearning upon his return.

"I am ready for you to take me above, my lord. I am ready to reach the highest level of light. I await for you to send me," she said, just as she pulled a sheet up to cover herself.

Mortifer walked over to a teapot that was kept heated by a single glowing candle and poured a cup of its brew. The liquid was thicker and darker than any coffee, and the scent was stiff and bitter. He then added a spoonful of sugar to the cup and stirred it.

"I am making you a cup of tea. It is a recipe we have used for thousands of years to help free the spirit from the flesh. Drink this if you truly wish to see your father. It goes down better if you drink it all at once."

The young girl took the cup and emptied the contents in two swallows, taking care not to stop for breath in between. By the look on her face, it was evident she did not care for the aftertaste.

"Lay back, let yourself be pleasured once again while the medicine takes hold," he said, and then gently pushed her backward to the bed.

She could feel herself becoming somewhat light headed. Her fingers and toes grew warm while her skin tingled uncontrollably. As he licked his way across her stomach and began kissing the inside of her thighs, her entire body became covered in goose bumps.

He gently went to work on her with his mouth, and within minutes she began quaking in the most intense pleasure she had ever known, far exceeding her own experience from just a few minutes before. It seemed every pore in her body had become an erogenous zone in and of itself.

As her ecstasy reached its apex, she could hardly breathe. She found herself unable to make a noise, and when he stopped, a rush of a thousand sensations washed over her. She shivered in a pleasure so vivid she became like a stone. Then, it seemed he simply let her lay there for an eternity.

Between the acrid opiate based tea taking effect, and the strange new erotica she had been introduced to, Mortifer had her in the exact frame of mind and body he wanted. He then picked her up, and carried her languid form into an adjacent room he called *the chamber*.

Inside the chamber it was dark, just a single candle burned in the corner, and the only piece of furniture she could see was of the most unusual design. It looked like a table, but one that was constructed of wood in such a way that it was clearly intended to support a human laying upon it. It was complete with shackles for binding wrists at the top and ankles toward the bottom.

In the center of the table, right where it would seem the legs of anyone laying would meet, there was a removable piece of wood with a peculiar groove cut into its center. The groove progressively got deeper toward the edge of the board, where there was a tin cup attached below. For the first time all evening, the young girl began to grow uncomfortable and frightened.

She could not move or speak. She felt the cold, flat wood against her bare skin. She felt the icy iron shackles as he placed them over her wrists and then her ankles. She wanted to scream out, but her voice failed her. She could feel herself breathing in and out, but she couldn't control the depth or the pace of it.

Mortifer positioned himself in front of her. His face was nothing like the playful and captivating man she began to love and trust only a short time before. His eyes widened. The white in his gaze had all but disappeared. His stare had become fully black, and it bordered on demonic. When he lined himself up, he took her by both shoulders, and...

Terror nearly stopped the girl's heart. She felt the flesh of her femininity torn violently, as if she were stabbed by a red hot piece of iron pulled straight from the coals. Her eyes instantly flooded with tears. She could hear the sound of her own blood collecting in the tin affixed beneath the grooved board. Even if she could cry out, it was unlikely she would have made much of a noise.

The look in her face begged of him, *why this?* The greater the horror in her eyes, the more bloodthirsty he became. She wanted to die, or at the least faint, but the strange concoction flowing in her veins would not permit her to do either. This exacting moment was precisely what Mortifer was after all along.

The terrified and confounded look in her eyes. The purity of her youth and innocence being torn away so savagely. He had been trained from a young age, by every advisor in the role now filled by Hadrian, to take the blood of a virgin girl and consume it. The rite's singular purpose served to retain his youth and vigor.

There was a time when he drugged the girls completely unconscious and bled them through the neck with a knife as they slept. At least they did not suffer then. But over the centuries, his vanity grew into a maliferous narcissism.

He genuinely came to believe that the blood collected at the very point of a girl's immaculate flesh being broken was more potent. He believed that as she bled out, he captured not just her cruor, but the essence of her innocence and naiveté. The fear and the adrenaline mixed with the blood only made it so much sweeter to the buds of his abhorrent tongue.

Mortifer assaulted her for nearly an hour, with each violent thrust more injurious than the one before, until at last he was spent and he lay nearly on top of her in a state of utter exhaustion. As he moved away, he gently kissed her cheek and her forehead to which she looked back at him in anguish, and in rage.

When Mortifer stepped back, he proudly examined the byproduct of his deeds. He stood there, watching, as the girl bled out in rhythm with the beat of her angry heart. The tin cup collecting her blood had nearly run over when all of a sudden, she let out the most somber and continuous wail he had ever heard.

At this, Jeringas Mortifer nearly went into a state of total panic. Never before had his strange opiate brew worn off before he could dispose of the girl he had taken. As she continued crying, her voice escalated, growing louder and louder. Mortifer feared the thought of any of his common servants running in to aid him. He knew if they learned the real secret behind The Day of Mirrors ritual, word could easily reach the outside. Then he might never find willing participants for the rite again.

Mortifer quickly returned to his bedroom and poured another cup of the potion. He ran back to the chamber and tried forcing more of the drink down the girl's throat, but she refused. She coughed it back in his face, and began to cry even louder.

Unwilling to risk contaminating the harvest he had yielded, he quickly removed the collection tin and set it out of the way. Mortifer then grabbed a large knife he kept nearby, just in case of the very event that was unfolding, and firmly placed it against her neck.

"Time for you to transcend, my dear girl." As he whispered into her ear, he drew the knife backwards, cutting deep into her throat.

"Shhhhh!" he calmly demanded, as the blade crunched through her trachea. "Shhhhh!" he demanded again, as he felt the steel drag into the bone of her neck.

Bright red blood flowed down the wooden table and cascaded over the edge like a waterfall. Her mouth gurgled ever so slightly while he tried to silence her. All the anguish and rage that had amassed within her eyes was quickly displaced by a remorseful consignment to her fate.

Mortifer quietly unshackled the girl and then carried her through a hidden door to a small terrace that was barely visible to anyone on the outside. The terrace faced a part of the moat in the rear of the fortress where there was very little in the way of light, and was generally left unguarded in the dark of night.

The young girl's eyes had closed. Most of the blood in her body had been emptied in one manner or another. He opened her eyes with his left hand and looked to see if there was any consciousness remaining within them.

He saw one last glimmer of recognition, so he ran the fingers of his right hand up her side, and forced her to watch as he licked them one by one.

"You were one of the sweetest I ever knew. Go now, and be with your father," said the king, ever so softly, and directly into her ear. He then rolled her spent body over the edge of the terrace, where she plunged some ninety feet to the watery surface below.

Her lifeless form floated there momentarily. Within seconds, the crocodiles moved in, each taking a limb into a death roll. As her body was shredded to pieces, all evidence of what transpired on this, the year's seventh Day of Mirrors, sank into the murky depths with the reptilian beasts.

Jeringas Mortifer calmly returned to the chamber, poured himself a glass of red wine, and drank the blood of his sacrifice slowly, savoring each mouthful as it went. With each gulp of blood, he chased it with another sip of the wine, until both cups were empty.

Jeringas Mortifer long held the belief that this very ritual is what kept his body young and powerful. He was only half immortal, and he feared his mortal half might one day begin to deteriorate. Yet as long as he performed the ritual, he never visibly aged. For over two millennia, he had practiced and perfected this rite.

He checked himself once more in the mirror. He then gathered the knife, the tin, the bleeding board, and returned to the bath where the water was still luke warm. He cleansed himself and all of his equipment. He was careful to wash away any indication of what had occurred. He stared silently as the pinkish red water emptied through the tub's drain. When it was done, he put the equipment back in the chamber, locked the door behind him, and piled the laundry for his servants to remove the following day.

The king could tell the sun would be rising before long. Most of the candles that lit his room during the night had already expired. So Jeringas Mortifer packed his pipe with fresh tobacco, poured himself a rather large glass of wine, and settled himself in bed for the remains of the morning darkness.

When he finished his smoke, and the wine finally pushed him to the brink of sleep, he found himself drifting into a dream of wide open fields, crisp fragrant breezes, and tall flowers dancing in euphony with the shifting winds.

He was barefoot. He could feel the softness of the grasses beneath his feet. His dreaming head swung from east to west. There, the field he found himself standing within seemed to span outward for miles and miles with no real end in sight. The flowers he envisioned were of too many different types to enumerate.

They were breathtaking, inspiring even, and every color in the known spectrum of light was well represented.

Every color but red.

CHAPTER SEVEN

DEVIL IN THE DARKNESS

It wasn't quite morning yet. Pieter had managed to shrug off the events of his day trip to San Kitts. He pushed the whole experience into some deep corridor within his mind where neither his wife nor his first mate could find any evidence of what transpired. Yet, as he slept, these mental doorways creaked back open, and he found himself dreaming of The Seer.

His first recollection of her in the dim lit room haunted him. Even as he slept, he deeply regretted seeing her natural form so unobstructed. He pondered whether it was possible for a man to be unfaithful by the actions of his eyes alone. His internal debate was ended suddenly, and without warning, when a visage of the devilish old woman entered his mind and overtook that of the alluring Seer. His mind quickly diverted away from the day before and centered on the present eve.

The ringing chimes outside woke him. He felt the air growing inexplicably cold around him. It was a chill unlike any he had felt since the late fall days in Amsterdam.

When he sat up, he looked around the room. It seemed Lauren was perfectly comfortable in her sleep. Pieter gently touched her forehead. By comparison, her skin was downright balmy. So he got up and walked over to the crib. Little Stephen was fast asleep, clutching his blue knitted blanket with his tiny hands. Pieter gently touched his head with the back of his fingers. The baby felt pleasingly warm to his touch.

Where did this confounding cold come from? Pieter wondered. *Am I getting ill?* He walked quietly into the main room with his arms crossed, shivering. Somewhere between the rustling leaves and ringing metal chimes, he thought he heard an unfamiliar voice in the distance. Pieter held his breath while he listened for it again.

Patris, it called. This time he understood it clearly. The voice was deep and flowed forth with a phrenic potency uncommon in normal men. Pieter looked to the door and saw his saber propped against the frame. He did not even remember bringing it into the house. Just as he reached for its hilt, a yellow flash of light caught the corner of his eye. When Pieter realized he could see his own breath, he knew something was terribly amiss.

He drew the saber from its scabbard and walked toward the glassless window where the strange light had flickered. He saw it again, but it had split into a pair of yellow bursts. The light seemed further away, but more intense than before. Pieter stared for a moment. Once he honed in on where the light was coming from, he crept out of the door to investigate.

Never before had Pieter so dearly wished that Franklin and his 'buss were right there with him. The ground beneath his bare feet seemed remarkably warm considering how cold the air was that wafted about him. As the wind whipped around a tall tree in the distance, he could barely make out the form that stepped out from beneath its branches. Pieter was not sure if it was a man or otherwise. The cape flowing behind the figure flapped like the wings of a massive bat against the night sky. Pieter looked behind himself. It was so dark, he could not see Franklin's house at all.

As the towering figure drew closer, Pieter still could not make out more than just an outline, its general shape.

"Stop where you are!" Pieter yelled. "Do not come closer! I am armed!" Pieter's voice rang aloud like pure steel. The towering figure halted his advance.

"*Patris*," it called again. As the air grew even more chilled, Pieter felt his muscles involuntarily firing and flexing, in an effort to combat the effects of the cold.

"I am neither your father nor a priest. Whatever you are, you will find no welcome here," said Pieter. This time, there was no immediate reply.

The air grew still as the fishing boat captain and the towering shadow stared back at one another. As Pieter squinted in the darkness, and tried to sharpen his sight, he could feel the stranger was sizing him up in return.

"*I like your spirit*," the massive figure said at last. "For now we cannot see one another. But you will see me soon enough, *Patris*." Pieter's eyes never wavered as he listened. He felt compelled to remain silent, as if saying anything at all might endanger his life or his family. But in his heart, he knew he couldn't just stand there.

Pieter leapt forth, with his blade drawn high, and violently slashed downward at the massive, towering human form. Certain his blade would connect with the imposing shadow man's torso, Pieter instead felt nothing, and nearly lost his balance on the follow through.

The tip of his saber struck down into the soil as the figure dissipated like a cloud of smoke caught in a gust of wind. When he regained his defensive posture, Pieter saw a flash of silver streaking toward him. Pieter swiftly moved his saber outward to parry the strike.

The blackened curved steel cracked loudly. Pieter's blade had been sheered completely free from its hilt, and he fell backward onto the ground in awe. The charcoal grey figure then rematerialized, standing right before him, and pointed a colossal Zweihander sword at Pieter's chin. When no finishing stroke came, Pieter slid backwards and sat more upright.

"This is not real," he whispered, as his eyes strained to gain focus on the apparition like being. The towering form slowly withdrew his blade and began backing away into the brush.

"It soon will be, Patris," the towering form replied.

"You had best hope not. Because if you see me again, it will be for the last time," answered Pieter, his voice brimming with confidence.

"That much is certain," the low voice growled in return. Pieter could barely make out the shape of a huge hand as it spread out. Then a bright blue light shot out from its palm and blinded him completely. Pieter closed his eyes, turned away from it, and the smothering chill in the air receded at once.

Pieter could still feel himself laying face down. He slowly opened his right eye. Even in the darkness, he could see the cradle across the room, hear his wife and child breathing softly. All that surrounded him was both familiar and comforting. He knew immediately that it had all been in a dream, that he never left his house, and there was no towering boogeyman hiding in the bushes outside.

Both his wife and baby were peacefully asleep. Yet Pieter couldn't help himself. He had to get up. So he walked to the main room of his house. His saber was not by the door. No, it was locked away on board the *Vissen*, right where he had left it, right where he always kept it.

I wonder if perhaps I ought to begin keeping some weapon in the house from this night forward? Pieter silently asked himself.

He looked across the way to Franklin's house. Nobody was awake yet. He stared out the window for a while and saw nothing, not one thing that might make him believe the dream was anything but a random, senseless play of the imagination. In one way, that bothered him even more.

Pieter did not have random, senseless dreams like that, not ever. He dreamed of huge fishing hauls. He dreamed of owning more boats and hiring the men he would need to run them. He dreamed of building a second floor to his house, of continuing to build on the new life he had started with his wife and son in this, the New World.

His dreams were always grounded in the things that were real to him. Even his sleepy recollection of The Seer didn't bother him quite so much once he was awake. She was real. He had actually met her. He also gathered he was not the first man to recall her striking form in his slumber. But in that moment, he lost all desire to go outside.

Somehow, through the open window, way beyond what he could see, even with the aid of a looking glass, he felt unwelcome eyes were searching for him. He could feel it, right to the core of his bones. He could feel those yellow eyes scanning out, possibly from hundreds of miles away even, but he knew them to be there.

Pieter wondered whose voice he had heard. He wondered how his mind, if it were only playing tricks, could invent the faceless, smoke-like apparition, without ever having seen something even remotely like it before.

So Pieter sat down in a chair, and though his eyes were growing heavy, he stared out the window into the great dark beyond, looking back at the source of the foreboding. His stare carried both the weight of caution and warning.

On the other side of the darkness, drifting northbound slowly on a starless night, the two mast, 120 foot schooner style boat *Unda Jaulaor* was sailing just beyond the view of Catia La Mar. A small, single mast scouting craft sailed out in front of her, while a pair of 60 foot cutters that served as supply gathering and messenger boats followed up the rear.

It was too dark to read any of the literature that Hadrian had assembled for him. The Soul Collector did not require sleep either. So, to pass the time, he stared into the great expanse of blackness ahead. With his own version of extra sensory perception, his own third eye of sorts, The Soul Collector scanned over the waves to the horizon above them. He knew his quarry was out there. He could almost see him as he called out the cryptic name in his mind.

Patris, he called outward with only his mind, almost as a whisper, but more like a telepathic growl. He thought for a moment he had made contact. In his mind, he thought he saw a man approaching him in the shadows of some random island village. But in the same instant it was blocked out again. Yet he heard a voice.

The accent was different, and difficult to identify. The man may have spoken English, but *he* was not English. He was definitely not French or Spanish. He was not a native islander either. He was something else. He was confident and strong, both willing and capable of defending his home. The Soul Collector couldn't see the man's face, but he sensed a great deal of honor and resolve within him.

It is often said that the fruit never falls far from the tree, he thought to himself. *This could be the father I will be charged with finding. I sense a respectable and worthy adversary. Just not tonight. Not yet.*

He had his orders. By his own suggestion to the king, The Soul Collector had no cause to seek the Child of Prophecy or the boy's family. Yet, he had a curiosity where the boy was concerned. The Soul Collector was in tune with the dark forces of the continuum like no other. He surmised his connection to the continuum of being surpassed that of Lord Mortifer himself. He was curious to learn whether his unique bond with the world abroad could lead him right to the ordained child's doorstep.

Shamans and vampires, he thought to himself. *Surely, it would be easier for me to find the boy? Surely, I of all beings, would be able to sense his presence?* The Soul Collector shook his head. He had his orders, and the crux of his arrangement with Mortifer was to follow them.

The Soul Collector moved to the bow and turned an empty wooden crate into a seat. While his form did not require the dormancy of sleep that humans did, he could shut out the world and sink his consciousness into a meditative like state. In the deep black of a night sky completely unbroken by light, he found the forward most point of his ship an ideal setting for just such a trance.

The winds were growing favorable, and the *Unda Jaulaor* was gathering speed on her heading north. The fluttering canvas, the murmur of the rising and falling sea, the tempo of his ship's keel as it repeatedly cut through the ocean froth, along with the cold indigo drape of eventide, together they completely enveloped him in spiritual harmony and cerebral concert. He could feel the dark powers of the continuum were smiling on him once again. He also felt that the light powers of the continuum sensed his advent. Though they would seek to impede him, he knew they trembled all the same.

He sensed that a new player had joined in the game of the lost prophecy. He long suspected The Order of the Third Eye would eventually find Azura's successor. He looked forward to the challenge of discovering who he or she might be. But, as he turned his head to the East, looking, feeling outward with his mind, he sensed nothing where the mysterious shaman known as Peiman was concerned. The Soul Collector only sensed that trouble was brewing, and it was due east from his current position.

He did not need a map to know the location. He knew based on his departure point, the time elapsed during travel, and the proximity of where the sensation was coming from, his mind was being drawn to Kairi and Bella Forma. He did not know exactly how or why. He just had an overwhelming sense of foreboding where the three islands of liberated slaves now resided.

But since his master seemed to have his own plans for handling them, The Soul Collector shifted his focus back to that which was directly ahead of him. The *Unda Jaulaor* and her sailing party were now heading on a straightaway that was less than twenty hours from Isla Mona. Once the sun rose, The Soul Collector would take up his reading about the Romanian *strigoi*.

In all his long years of being, he had heard whispers of their existence, but he had never actually seen a vampire, no matter what name it might have gone by. Given his former occupation, and for how long he was procured as such, he found their existence highly unlikely. Because if anyone were to meet one, or confirm their deeds via the dead, he was at the very forefront of the shortest list to have done so.

He found the prospect of going to an island inhabited entirely by the undead both grisly and fascinating. Regardless of whatever literature Hadrian assembled, the Soul Collector prepared to be surprised.

So he drew his thoughts inward, and ceased thinking outward across the winds and rippling water. He stilled his mind and rested his body. He put forth no abnormal forms of mental or spiritual energy that might be detected by the more psychically inclined. After all, once he arrived on Isla Mona, he was certain the strigoi were going to be of some surprise to him. He figured the least he could do was return the favor.

CHAPTER EIGHT

UNCOMMON PROGRESS

Off the island of Camahogne, a land today known as Grenada, in the harbor of the abandoned slave trading port the Spanish called La Bay, an assortment of sailing vessels was gathering just before mid day. The ships were mostly remnants of the Spanish armada, abandoned after their brief attempt to colonize Kairi and Bella Forma, and ranged from single mast dinghies all the way up to huge, three mast galleons. All of them were commandeered by the former slaves who recently gained their independence.

Regardless of how they came to be free, the three islands gained their freedom in sudden fashion. Herein lay the problem. No one among their ranks actually planned to achieve such rapid liberty. Nobody was prepared for the weight that came with such a massive shift of responsibility. Camahogne had been free for roughly half a year while Kairi and Bella Forma gained their independence barely more than a month before.

Even among the Africans, the residents of the three islands faced serious linguistic challenges. The slave trade was indiscriminate. Men, women, and children were abducted from all over the African continent. For every elder that rose up as a leader, he or she needed a translator who could understand a dozen different dialects or languages. And, in the midst of all three islands were small populations of both Carib and Arawak natives who had been displaced by the Spaniards.

In the wake of the Spanish withdrawal from the islands, practically everyone saw themselves becoming a head of state in one form or another. But without the backing of a major European power, nobody wanted to assume the mantle of leadership, not with the threat of Jeringas Mortifer standing right on their collective doorstep.

Camahogne as a community was the most united of the islands, and its leadership the most purposeful. So the elders of Camahogne invited every tribal leader from Kairi and Bella Forma to meet in La Bay and discuss their collective future.

Several of the visiting tribal heads felt a great sense of distrust towards Camahogne and its burgeoning government. They had all heard of Peiman, the mystical Arawak shaman who came and went at will. While the Africans of Camahogne saw him as a wise old partner, and the spiritual leader of a revolution against enslavement, others saw him as a potentially manipulative influence. After all, he was a native of the Windward Islands. Many of his kind had been killed or driven off their ancestral lands. It was only natural that some of the recently freed slaves wondered openly about his interests.

Perhaps their greatest cause for concern was the brash young Englishman, the former major of the British army, Adam Tyre. In a matter of months, he had managed to implement many English practices and cultures on Camahogne.

He enlisted privateers to aid him in establishing, and continually training two branches of military; an army and a navy. Major Tyre had also recruited a number of teachers to set up an education system. He even bribed a few European landowners into giving up some indentured field hands to help Camahogne establish a variety of productive food crops.

The creation of a defense system, formal education, advances in agriculture; these things would usually be a welcome addition to a land that otherwise would have none of the aforementioned. Except in this case, the chief architect behind these developments was a white man.

When some of the tribal leaders from Kairi and Bella Forma heard that many of their African brethren of Camahogne went so far as to adopt English names, they stopped just short of calling it treason against their own people. Perhaps because they did not understand why.

The delicate task of general enlightenment was left in the careful hands of three men who had adopted just such names. Lionel Brown was a big man in his early forties, and many considered him to be Camahogne's ultimate authority. He was around six feet four inches tall, with broad shoulders, cannon ball biceps, and powerful legs.

His skin was dark, even for an African, and his facial features were well pronounced. He wore a beard that he kept perpetually well groomed. His eyes were dark brown and permanently serious. Most every woman who had ever met him considered him to be very handsome. Not only was Lionel Brown a leading man in local politics, he was the lone general of Camahogne's army.

Sigmond Wright was a thinner man, almost as tall as General Brown, and around fifty years in age. His hair was spotted with gray, and his complexion was rather light. He originally came from a region of Africa where he might very well have had some Egyptian blood in his lineage.

His nose and mouth were relatively narrow. He was clean shaven, except for a beard he grew downward on his chin, in the shape of an inverted funnel. Some of his friends jokingly called him 'pharaoh,' given his resemblance to paintings of the ancient Egyptian rulers. He was a great thinker, something of a wise man among his kind, and quite skilled in the art of persuasion. Most of Camahogne considered Sigmond to be General Brown's intellectual counterpart and political equal.

Andre Washington was the youngest of the three. He was only in his early twenties, of average height, and average build. He kept his hair short and wore a goatee. His eyes were light brown, while his expression was always kind and intelligent. He was the most charismatic of the three, and many considered Andre to be the future of Camahogne's leadership.

He had gained some notoriety because he volunteered to take his father's place when the slave traders came to his homeland back in Africa. Yet he never accepted the label of hero. Andre had a half dozen younger siblings, and he was already a grown man at the time. He simply believed he and his family would be better served if he took his father's place on a slave ship as opposed to the head of the family. He was a deeply spiritual man, extremely committed to his beliefs and values, and he firmly believed he would find his destiny at the far end of his journey across the sea.

As fate would have it, Andre Washington was among the first to meet Peiman. He was at the very heart of the slave uprising once the lost prophecy was made known to him. Being an exceptional learner, he easily absorbed Peiman's teachings regarding the continuum, the Hallowed Guardians, the Primeval Scourges, the true nature of Jeringas Mortifer, and the Child of Prophecy.

So great was Andre Washington's faith in the destiny unfolding before him, he joined General Brown's army despite never having wielded a weapon in his life. Driven by the passion of his belief, he soon became exceptionally skilled in combat by hand, by the sword, and with the primitive firearms of the day. He was a natural at sailing and a brilliant tactician. After rapidly ascending the ranks of both the army and navy, he was given the ubiquitous position known as the Master at Arms.

The largest structure in La Bay was a stone fort that overlooked the harbor. The fort had been completed literally days before the Spaniards withdrew from the island. The stones they used to complete it were bright white, and hardly looked weathered at all. In a word, it looked new.

On the second floor, there was a great hall that had been set up like an auditorium. It was relatively wide open, with huge gaps in between thick stone columns to provide light and allow fresh air to pass freely. Here, the tribal leaders and their companions gathered in an orderly fashion.

General Brown, Sigmond Wright, and Andre Washington were all seated at a table near the front of the room, facing the crowd. Most notably absent were Major Tyre and Peiman. They were nowhere to be seen. Other than a couple guards standing at the entrance, there was very little in the way of an armed presence.

Sigmond Wright kept a close watch on the door, and kept his ears tuned in to the mood of the crowd. As fewer and fewer people joined, the group became a seated mass of mumbles and whispers of various tongues, with the occasional chuckle thrown in. Except for the three men at the head of the room, who were all dressed in their military attire, there was little uniformity at all.

Some of the tribal leaders wore brightly colored tunics, others wore elaborate head dresses but no shirt, while some remained in the same garb provided by their captors when they first arrived in the New World as slaves.

Sigmond appreciated and understood the diversity of his people. After all, there were thousands of tribes on his home continent. But what he had hoped to see was some interaction among the various groups, some sign of unity other than the color of their skin. As he observed the crowd, he only saw each little faction ignoring the next. Even though he largely expected this to be the case, he couldn't help but feel just a little disappointed. After fifteen minutes or so passed without anyone else entering, General Brown called the meeting to order.

At first, it seemed that nothing would successfully be discussed, let alone get accomplished. It took the tribal leaders fifteen minutes just to agree on two translators, as there wasn't a single member of the crowd who could fluently speak every language in use. Trust of the translators was scarce to begin with. None of the men wanted to be misrepresented or misunderstood.

It took another twenty minutes for the two dozen or so tribal leaders to identify themselves and their place of origin. While General Brown seemed to find the whole activity somewhat amusing, Sigmond Wright became increasingly impatient. So he stood up and took the lead from General Brown and addressed the group in Spanish, the one language that everyone seemed to know at least a fragmented version of.

"Brothers of Africa," he began. "We are joined here today, I hope, in friendship. But at the least we should all recognize the common past that binds us." Sigmond spoke slowly and deliberately. He allowed several pauses between sentences for the translators to catch up.

"Very few of us knew one another in our homeland across the sea. But we know one another now. We have far more in common than what we hold to be different. We are all men taken from our homes, from family, from freedom, made into slaves of labor, until the time came that we could take our freedom back. Now it is time to decide what to do with this gift of freedom, of life, of a future that is up to us to decide. I have only a few words to offer. I speak on behalf of my co-council, Mr. Washington and Mr. Brown. But first, I wanted to address some of the more unpleasant rumors that are about."

"First and foremost, we have no desire to make war with any African, or any former slave for that nature. That would include the native people of these lands, and even some of the white men that choose to live here." At his last remark, there were a few understated gasps and comments. Sigmond only paused briefly enough to allow the chatter to die off.

"The army and navy we have formed are both strictly for defense purposes. You must understand what it is that we wish to defend against. The men who once enslaved us, they did not see us as other men, as people. They saw us as property, as beasts of burden, and we each had a price, a value. Men such as these do not leave chests of treasure buried in the sand with the intent of forgetting them."

"No, these men, we believe they will come back one day. Whether to seize us as property, or to avenge those that were killed, or to take back the lands we have worked. There is good reason to expect and fear their return. So we, the free people of Camahogne, we have taken it upon ourselves to build our own army and our own navy. Whether by force, or just the threat of force, we will repel any man of any origin who might come to enslave us again. Yet we will also welcome any man of any origin who seeks to be our friend and ally. We offer our services to the recently liberated peoples of Kairi, and of Bella Forma. We will gladly train your willing men, so you may make your own armies, your own navies. So we ask you; join us, as allies and bothers, because surely, you fear the same things that we do. I will now invite your feedback and questions. I only ask that we speak one at a time, and please rise so we all can hear you."

After Sigmund spoke, the group was initially silent and still. Finally, one older man in the rear of the room stood up. He was wearing an orange tunic, and a simple hat made of black cotton, and went by the name of Abasi.

"My brother," he began. His voice was soft and dry sounding, the hurt of his brutal past clung deeply to his vocal chords.

"I believe what you say about the white men returning. I think many of us have privately worried about the same thing in our beds at night." As he paused to clear his throat, most every one of the tribal leaders nodded in agreement.

"But we are all troubled by the English major who lives among you. Your people might respect him. Your people might even welcome him. But to many of us, as far as we are concerned, he is just another white devil. Plenty of English men bought slaves from the Spanish. This makes their kind just as guilty." As Abasi sat down, the mumbling in the room grew louder, the nodding more expressed. Sigmond held up his hands to quiet the room.

"Major Tyre came to us as a friend, and he is a friend. He has his reasons to help us, and he has helped us immensely. He has never been part of the problem. He has never owned a slave. No one in his bloodline has ever owned a slave," Sigmond responded in a kind tone.

A younger man known as Thabo, immediately rose to his feet. He was dressed in a more elaborate black tunic with gold stitching, and his intricate necklace made from polished bones and seashells jingled as he moved.

"And what about his friends? We hear there are many white people on your island now. It seems they are running your whole country." The young man's voice was angry and high pitched. As he carried on, the more the crowd seemed to stir in agreement.

"They are the ones teaching your armies how to fight? Why? The only time your people fought the whites, the whites lost! They are the ones teaching your children in these so called schools? They are teaching your people how to farm the lands, to gather water, and breed birds? Didn't we learn all of these things back home? We don't want these white people. We don't need them. It smells of betrayal! It smells like they are only training your people to improve their lot when they sell you back to the

Spaniards. I would rather cut off the hand of any white man who extends it before I take it in mine. I spit at the thought!"

And spit on the ground, Thabo did, as the crowd around him grew positively boisterous. Sigmond tried to regain control of the group with some calm hand gesturing, but his efforts were futile.

General Brown stood up, and as he did, he picked up one end of the table he was sitting at. He lifted the table end up about three feet off the ground and let it slam down loudly against the stone floor. With one look into his dark and captivating eyes, the crowd immediately became seated and silent.

"You there, stand up," said General Brown, as he pointed directly at Thabo. The general then beckoned him to the front of the room. "Stay here for a moment," added the general, who disappeared outside for a couple of minutes.

When he returned, he brought Major Tyre back in with him. The general then walked over to the young tribal leader and handed him a long wooden spear, not unlike one that Thabo would have used back in their homeland of Africa. The spear was made of a sturdy piece of decorated wood, and featured a serrated stone cutting head that could easily kill a wildebeest.

"Major Tyre, please extend your hand in friendship to this young man." The major quietly did as he was ordered. General Brown then turned to Thabo.

"There he is, your *white devil*. Go ahead. Cut off his hand, or his head, whatever you prefer. He is right there. Go on!" barked the general.

The young man stared blankly at the major. The major was not yet twenty-five but his hairline was already receding. He was a fairly robust man, equally powerful as he was tall, and slightly thick in the middle. He had a close cut goatee and his dark blue uniform was steeped in regal authority. Thabo ground his teeth at the sight of the major, but refused to advance.

"What are you waiting for? Go on!" General Brown insisted.

"He has a gun!" the young man replied at last, pointing to major's pistol. "Let me drop this spear, and he his arms, and then we'll fight," Thabo added.

"Oh, I see. Because when the Spanish return, they will leave their guns and their swords behind. Because that is how they have conquered almost a third of the known world, by being fair minded in battle," quipped the general. The young tribal leader lowered his spear and stared at the floor in shame.

General Brown extracted the major's curved saber from its scabbard. With two quick slashes, the general proceeded to cut the spear head from the pole in Thabo's hands, and then hacked another third of the shaft away just for effect.

When he was done, the general pointed the saber at Thabo's head in perfect British saber fighting form. The young man instantly dropped the remains of the wooden spear and put his hands up in surrender.

"Didn't you say we would be fine without the white man? Then why didn't you defeat me with the spear and your skill? I heard you were a very good warrior, one of the best in your village back home," said the general. Thabo did not seem inclined to reply in any manner at all.

"This, my brothers, is why we cannot entirely rely on what we learned from our fathers long ago. This young man was afraid of the major's gun. The major didn't even need to draw it. This steel sword was all I needed to defeat a wooden spear. On this side of the world, there is no white or black in war... or in living. There are only better ways and lesser ways of getting things done. You cannot beat a sword with a wooden spear. Do they teach us how to fight? Yes. But more importantly, they are teaching us how to *win* a fight against our former captors, should they ever return. Do they teach us how to dig wells and find water, without having to walk for miles to a river? Yes. If that is such a bad thing, I demand an explanation as to why." General Brown paused for a moment.

"Do they teach us how to speak their tongues? Yes, and why not? My father spoke twelve languages. He learned many different tongues so he could trade with many neighboring tribes. I would think I am honoring the memory of my father by educating myself at least as well. Have they taught us to farm? Not entirely. Most of us already knew how to grow a crop or two. But we are learning to take advantage of the many wild spices that grow here, plants we would not have identified or even known to be valuable without the major's people. And, we are already making friends and allies with those who wish to buy the spices from us. We all learned something from someone else. A man once learned to make fire, then taught it to ten others, who taught it to ten others. Then another man learned to cook meat with the fire, and so on.

This is not about the color of skin. This is about progress." The general paused once again, and looked about the room for any reaction.

"You hate the white man. I will not insult you and pretend you have no reason for this hatred. But I have heard that many of your people are entertaining the idea of going home. I have no doubt you could build a big enough boat and sail it safely across the sea. But I will not lie to myself, or my people, about what awaits us there. I will not forget Lomboko. I will not forget how I got there. You..." The general pointed back to Thabo once more as he continued.

"I knew your King Sizwe." Thabo's eyes widened, and he stood up straighter when the general mentioned the name of his former king.

"Your king sold you and hundreds of your people out. I never once saw a Spaniard any deeper inland than the coast at Lomboko. No, the Spaniards paid your king, they paid all of our kings, and their princes, with heavy sacks of gold, to send their own soldiers, *black* soldiers, into the mainland and take us. You can hate the white man. You can blame him to your heart's eternal satisfaction. But it was also our own kind who sold us into slavery. Some say if they had not sold us, the Spaniards, with their modern weapons, might have killed our kings and their families. We can debate forever whether they had much of a choice. But one thing is clear. I never knew one of our kings who chose to stand and fight for us instead of taking the easy way out. I never knew one chief who chose us, his own people, over a big payment of gold. Sure, if there had never been buyers of slaves, there would never have been a slave trade. But in the end, history will show there were evil men involved in these evil deeds of every color, including our own."

At this remark, most of the room stood up and began firing obscenities of every dialect at the general. But a few of the men, mostly the older ones, the ones who had spent real time in the slave prison known as Lomboko, they stayed seated.

After several minutes, the orange clad tribal elder at the rear of the room stood up again. The younger men took notice of the tears welling in Abasi's eyes, and out of respect, they all became seated and quiet once again.

"What the general says is true. I spent two years in Lomboko. I saw how the trade worked with my own two eyes. I was made to do things to my brothers and sisters with these hands I will forever regret. I am afraid we will not have a home there should we go back." Abasi's voice cracked as he spoke, and he had to sit down before he was emotionally overcome.

"Most of our villages have been wiped out," Sigmond interjected. "Many of the people we once loved have either been taken away, driven off, or killed. We might find our villages again. But they will be empty. And if our kings and tribal chiefs learn of our return, as free men, they will fear the knowledge we now have. They would not want us traveling through the woods and the jungles and the savannahs warning the other tribes and villages. They would fear their own people rising up against them. And, they would fear reprisals from the Spanish should any of them recognize us. Just by being there, it would make our people appear to be in league with us and our revolution.

No, our former kings and chiefs would sooner see us dead. If we go back, we will be hunted like wild animals until we are either killed, or trapped and sold back into slavery. Here, we are the rulers of our land. Here, we have no kings, no chiefs, no masters. Here, we choose who will lead us when we need them to. And here, we choose to what place they will lead us to. We, the free peoples of Camahogne, have decided. We are staying here. We are staying free."

Sigmond returned to his seat behind the table, and for a while, the tribal leaders and their translators talked among themselves. Sigmond's hopes began to rise as some of the older men in the rear of the room moved forward, and joined the discussions with the younger men up front. Emotions were kept in check. The dialogue was serious, but cordial and thoughtful. As the chatter died back down, Abasi walked to the front of the room and addressed both the crowd, and the three men at the table.

"We have agreed to stay. We will take this message to our people. We will stay and build a new life together. Should any of our people wish to go back to Africa, we will not stop them, but we will discourage it the best we can. We now wish to hear from Major Tyre. We want to know why he has chosen his current position, and come to live among us, in his words." The orange clad tribal elder was about to go back to his seat when he heard a most unexpected word.

"Stay," said Major Tyre, but in perfect Swahili, Abasi's native language. "Please," added the Major, once again, in perfect Swahili.

Abasi nodded in wondrous agreement, staring back at the young officer with curious eyes.

"My father was once a slave," the major began, this time in Spanish. Several men in the room gasped in disbelief. The statement seemed impossible.

"We had a different name for it. My father sold himself into servitude. You will find this is common among the white settlers here. Many cannot afford passage to the New World, so they sell themselves into servitude. But it is slavery all the same. There are young men out there on the islands right now who more or less belong to the landowners. In some cases, they take on a debt they will never repay, at least not in this lifetime. They work until the debt is repaid or pardoned. In my father's case, he sold himself into servitude before I was born. He died when I was just fifteen. The landowner took my mother to our magistrate, and they ruled that I would work in my father's place until his debt was repaid. I was only a boy. But I had no choice. If I refused, my mother, my little sisters and brothers, we all would have been evicted from the land and then thrown in a debtor's prison. So I agreed."

The major paused for a moment to clear his throat, and when he looked around the room, he could see the men were beginning to relate to his story.

"And I worked like a slave for two years until luck would find me one winter. I was out repairing a fence on a warm January afternoon when I heard a strange racket in the distance. I watched as a nobleman's carriage got hung up on a bridge crossing over a swollen stream. His horses panicked, and as they pulled themselves free from the carriage, the old wooden bridge collapsed. The nobleman was able to jump from the wreckage to the shore, but his son was thrown from the carriage into the frigid water."

"The nobleman let out a bloody terrible scream over his boy. The stream was overflowing with melting snow and moving fast. But I was far enough downstream to make a dash for the water, and jump in ahead of the boy. I was a good swimmer, but the cold of the water, it nearly took my breath the instant I plunged in. I had been in that stream a thousand times as a boy, but on that day, I was terrified it might be my last. I was able to swim against the current just enough to grab the boy. Then I turned and swam towards a low hanging tree branch. The boy was barely awake, but he had enough strength in him to hold onto me for dear life. Once I grasped the branch I was able to pull us both from the water and back to the shore."

"The little boy held fast to my chest whilst I raced up the muddy bank to the path that followed my master's fence line. I knew if I did not keep running, the cold would stop my heart. The nobleman had not seen me go in after the boy. He was kneeling and weeping at the sight of the wreck. When he saw me with the boy, his tears turned to pure joy. He wrapped the boy in his coat, and together we hurried to my mother's house for warmth. My brothers were sent to corral his escaped horses. Once the little boy had recovered well enough to travel, the nobleman took one horse to return home and left the other with me. He promised to return for the other horse the next day."

"He was back the next morning, bright and early. He brought a crew of twenty men to replace the old wooden bridge. He sought out my master, and paid off my father's debt. He also bought the land we tilled and had it titled to my mother. He then arranged for me to enter the military academy. He never did claim the other horse. I knew in that moment how lucky I was. I knew I was destined to help others improve their lot in life. So I was glad to receive a proper education and then join the army. I knew somewhere along the way, being in the military would offer me the chance to do some good. I never imagined that chance would come so far from home, but here we are. Here we have a chance to build a better country. Here we have a chance to make a place where more than just the nobles and the elite can prosper. I am proud to serve General Brown, far more proud than I was to serve my own country. He has my sworn allegiance. If your men were to join the army, they will have my allegiance as well."

At the conclusion of the major's speech, the room remained quiet. Abasi stood and nodded slowly to the major.

"Your story is one that is, sadly, too common. I did not know white slaves existed," said Abasi.

"By the thousands," replied the major.

"You could have chosen any rank when you joined this army. Why did you choose to be a major?" asked Sigmond, for the benefit of the room.

"I was a major when I resigned my original post. I only asked to keep the rank I had earned. And I will not ascend to a higher rank until I have earned a promotion. General Brown will not have it any other way. Neither will I," answered the major.

Abasi sat down in the middle of the room, while the other tribal leaders huddled around him. For a moment, it appeared matters were beginning to deteriorate once again, as translators and chiefs alike began to squabble over minor differences. But in short order, Abasi made his point to the other men, and they quieted down as the elder stood up amongst them.

"We will be proud to send our warriors to serve with General Brown and Major Tyre." As the words left Abasi's mouth, the entire room united in roaring applause. Major Tyre saluted the crowd, swiftly turned toward the door, and marched out.

In the immediate aftermath, there was a lot of hand shaking and delightful faces. But the young tribal head, Thabo, drifted toward the front of the room, with a bit of confusion in his expression. He held up his hands in the manner Sigmond had done earlier in the day, quietly asking for silence, and the room soon obliged.

"I am glad we have come to this agreement today. I believe we made our people stronger. But I was hoping to meet the medicine man, Peiman. I know many of us wanted to hear more about his prophecy, the one that so greatly inspired our brothers here on Camahogne, and led us all to freedom." As Thabo commented, both Sigmond and Lionel looked to the end of the table at Andre Washington, who was feverishly scribbling some notes.

Andre was not aware that all eyes had turned to him. Sigmond cleared his throat loudly.

"I believe Andre Washington can speak on Peiman's behalf," said Sigmond. Andre's attention quickly changed at the sound of his name.

"Yes, yes, my apologies, gentlemen." Andre began. His voice was even pitched, both authoritative and intellectual.

166

"I regret to inform you that Peiman could not be here for the gathering today. But he has promised to return at a later date, very soon I should say. He has to tend to his studies and meditation for now, but he has agreed to accompany me to Kairi in the near future. He is gathering all that he knows of the lost prophecy in order to share it with you. When he arrives on Kairi, we should plan a grand feast in his honor. By nightfall, we will put the children to bed and build a bonfire. You will not want to miss this. He will enlighten you in ways my words are not fit to describe." Andre could see the group was largely disappointed.

"Be ready in three days." Andre added, and the room's collective mood immediately improved.

"And what about the evil one? The terrible king they call Mortifer? What are we to decide about him?" Thabo asked.

"I don't know what there is to discuss, really," replied Andre. "Peiman's insight into the black king is invaluable. You will learn much about Lord Mortifer from the prophecy. Otherwise, we see him as just another threat to our freedom, no different than the Spaniards. We know he is ruthless. He enslaves those he conquers. He kills those he cannot. He is a wicked man and we stand ready to fight him the moment he chooses to attack," Andre added. General Brown joined his Master at Arms and continued where Andre left off.

"By the strength of our three islands, now united, we will soon have a mobile fighting force approaching twenty thousand men. Not even the mighty European powers can claim to have an army of such size anywhere in the Caribbean. We have all heard the rumors. We watch the

Dragon's Mouth night and day. We have seen ships with black sails come and go. There is a small wooden fort now across the strait, and a small gathering of tents, and little else that is new. I would think if Mortifer were serious about invading, he would have built a more permanent structure there," said General Brown. The crowd quietly nodded at the general's last remark.

"But make no mistake, he is a danger. We believe he intends to conquer this side of the world in its entirety. He will come for our lands eventually. Those that follow him, they are inspired by him, even willing to die for him. It might be six months. It might be a year. It might be six years. We know the black king will come for these lands at some point. But the longer he waits, the better it is for us. As we train our men, and build our boats, and grow our crops, and trade our goods for steel, we make ourselves ever a thicker shield against the mighty sword of Mortifer. We will be ready when he comes, and we will make him regret it."

At General Brown's last remark, the men in the assembly sprang up and roared aloud in confident applause and smiling approval.

"This concludes our meeting today. To those of you returning home by ship, be safe upon the seas. Keep the faith and spread the word," added Sigmond.

When the wooden doors in the rear opened, one by one, every man in the room made their way to the front. Each one shook the hand of Sigmond, General Brown, and the Master at Arms, Andre Washington. As they filed out, Major Tyre stood just outside with a guard on either side of him. The major held a lengthy salute to the tribal leaders as they walked back towards the harbor, while Sigmond kept a close eye on the interactions.

Abasi, the eldest of the tribal leaders, slowly shuffled his feet toward the major. Sigmond watched in amazement as the older man stood up straight, as much as his aging and aching back would allow, and crisply saluted the young major in return.

Abasi then asked the major to kneel. Major Tyre happily indulged. Lionel and Andre joined Sigmond in a quiet wonder at the spectacle. Together they watched as a tired, aging black man, a former slave, performed a blessing in the religion of his forefathers on a young, white, Christian born, former officer of the British king's army.

This, the three men knew, was so much deeper than cordial formality. It was beyond evident in Major Tyre's face that he was deeply touched and honored by the event. When the elder Abasi completed the blessing, it were as though a lifetime of anger had been shed from his skin. His hatred and hurt began crumbling to the ground like he was shedding a scaly hide made of flint rock.

At last, when the major looked up, young Thabo was standing at Abasi's side. Thabo knelt down to Major Tyre's level and offered his hand. The major took it with the apprehension of a stranger. When Thabo rose, he also pulled the major back to his feet. Then, once the young tribal leader released the major's hand, he crisply saluted him with a brief smile, and then loaned the elder Abasi his arm on their way back to harbor.

CHAPTER NINE

ISLA MONA

The *Unda Jaulaor* had made excellent time. The travel from Catia La Mar spanned some five hundred miles, yet The Soul Collector and his company arrived in under thirty-six hours. But rather than land immediately, they lowered their sails and remained adrift, almost out of view against the horizon.

Since their arrival placed them off the coast of Isla Mona just past mid day, The Soul Collector chose to read through his footnotes and marked pages one more time. He found the literature curious, extraordinary in some parts, but generally far fetched, even if his own king previously declared otherwise.

A strigoi most often has red hair and blue eyes, regardless of what its natural coloration may have been in life, he read silently to himself.

The strigoi is a shape shifter, and can transform itself into a variety of animals, such as owls, bats, rats, wolves, snakes, and spiders. The Soul Collector looked outward to the island in amazement.

"How could such a dynamic and talented creature escape my path through all the ages?" he asked aloud.

A strigoi is cunning, intelligent, not fond of daylight, and an expert at avoiding detection. At this, The Soul Collector paused.

"Well, if they can become something as common as a rat, that would certainly make one an expert at hiding in plain view, and a valuable agent of espionage," he commented to himself.

The strigoi do not live in populated areas and rarely socialize outside of their order. Given their nature, that they must feed on human blood to survive, they have been forced to largely live as

172

outcasts. The Soul collector paused once more. The comment brought to his mind the Day of Mirrors rite.

"I wonder if Jeringas Mortifer is not somehow related to these beings. Perhaps that is how he knew they were here, and I did not," he said, with a dun chuckle.

They typically reside in the darkest places. Abandoned crypts and dungeons are their preferred habitat. However they also find natural dwellings, such as caves, to be suitable. The strigoi are immortal in the sense that there is no known natural cause to their demise. If left to their own devices, it is widely believed they will continue on for eternity. However, there are some known methods of dispatching a strigoi to the netherworld. For the average man, the best method involves catching a strigoi off guard, such as when it sleeps, and then driving a stake made of ash through its heart.

"I suspect this would pretty much kill any known creature," The Soul Collector commented in a light hearted amusement.

The strigoi are exceptionally strong, often described as having the strength of ten or more men. They can leap incredible distances. They are faster than mortal men, but not as fast as a man on horseback. However, their stamina is almost without limit. An enraged strigoi was once reported to have tracked down a man over several miles and killed him after his horse was forced to pause for breath. Given all this, the best known defense against an attacking strigoi is decapitation. To prevent the strigoi from rising again, the head should be buried apart from the body, or the remains burned entirely.

"I should think the latter might be a bit extreme, if not time consuming," The Soul Collector quietly considered.

He then checked the sharpness of his pole arm's hewing blade.

"But decapitation... that should be a fairly easy remedy to apply to whatever trouble they might bring," he added, just as he set his weapon aside.

The strigoi have a hierarchy, of which little is known. It is said there is always one apex strigoi, such as a king or queen, and to eradicate the colony, the apex strigoi must be destroyed. The strigoi can multiply through typical, if not demonic, reproductive copulation. The strigoi also recruit new members through biting a normal human in the neck, and only draining part of the blood. If the strigoi were to drain the blood of the human entirely, the human is typically left permanently dead. However, when bitten and drained of blood entirely by an apex strigoi, for a period believed to be forty days, the apex strigoi may yet summon its victim to rise from the dead in its service. At this, The Soul Collector closed the book and began pacing the bow.

"Damián!" he called aloud.

Among The Soul Collector's six personal bodyguards, Damián was considered the group's leader. All of The Soul Collector's elite bodyguards were tall by the standard of their race, Muisca, but Damián was half Spaniard, and something of a giant at three inches past six feet. He had long and wavy brown hair, striking dark eyes, and a perpetual five o'clock shadow that just seemed to belong on his jaw line. He was handsome, well built, resourceful and intelligent. There was little mystery as to why The Soul Collector appointed him second in command.

"Yes, master," Damián answered upon arrival.

"We have only a matter of hours before sundown. I want to arrive on shore while there is still some daylight.

We only have an approximate idea of where the caves we seek are located. We need torches, one for every man, a couple of shovels, and I want every soldier equipped with a good wooden spear. Make certain the spears are solid wood, no stone or metal tips. Every man must also carry a good side sword. Pick two crossbowmen. Have them carve down some wooden stakes to about 18 inches or so, and make them as thick as can reasonably be fired. They will not need much range, but you will want them to penetrate a rib cage from up to 25 feet away. Make a few dry runs and test fire them into some water barrels if you must," The Soul Collector ordered.

"Understood, master," Damián responded.

"Once you have completed this task, I will advise you and your men further. But for now, make it clear that I must be in the lead when we land, when we explore, the entire time we walk that island. These men, including you, must put aside their loyalty and their instinct to aid me. If even half of what I have read about these creatures is true, then I am likely the only one among us who can survive a surprise strigoi attack. It would be better for me to draw them out and have the rest of you at the ready, to actually see what is coming," The Soul Collector warned. Damián smiled knowingly.

"It would be better for them if they just accepted your offer from Lord Mortifer. All will be done as you command, master."

As Damián departed, The Soul Collector gathered his thoughts and took measure of the sun's position in the sky above. He was more than ready. He was almost eager to get his mission underway.

As the sun encroached upon the western horizon, the *Unda Jaulaor* raised her black canvas sails and approached Isla Mona from the south. The Soul Collector briefed his men, and then timed their arrival with the setting sun to near perfection. There was no port, no docking station to speak of. So the *Unda Jaulaor* had to anchor off shore.

The Soul Collector and his small squadron of men piled into a pair of row boats and headed toward land just as the clouds above blossomed into various shades of orange, red and violet. The Soul Collector wasn't a fan of anything colorful, but away from the constant charcoal skies that lingered over the mainland south, he couldn't help but admire the different shades of light. The very nature of a sunset in this part of the Caribbean was different. His men, with their upward gazes, certainly took notice as well.

"Master, look, there!" called Damián, as he pointed towards a high cliff face just ahead.

When The Soul Collector focused his vision, he could clearly make out the dark entrances of what appeared to be caves.

"Correct your course slightly northwest," The Soul Collector commanded.

As soon as the rowers responded, and the two small boats changed direction, a colony of bats came screaming from out of the caves and headed above the cliff face to the center of the island.

"Master, you don't suppose that..." As soon as Damián spoke, The Soul Collector waved him off.

"I do suppose. Correct course back to original heading. And row faster." This time, the order came quietly, if not more sternly.

"Make land as soon as possible. We have to find a way up to the top that the men can swiftly retreat back down from. We'll be quicker on foot." The Soul Collector himself then moved to the rear of the boat, took up a pair of oars, and began pushing the boat ahead in unison with the men.

The last light was beginning to fade when they pulled the two small boats up onto the sand. The Soul Collector's keen eyesight spotted a meandering path through the stones that looked like nature's very own stairway to high ground.

"Light your torches, but keep them out of view until I've reached the top. From there, stay back on the trail, out of view. I assure you all that I will never be in danger. But I have no way of knowing if this vampirism is caused by some disease. If one of you contracts it, I cannot allow you to bring it back to Caracas. I will be forced to eliminate you. Is that understood?" The Soul Collector's company all nodded in agreement. "I will know more very shortly. If I am in need of your company, I will retreat here."

The towering figure then moved to the front of the formation, and began scaling his way up the jagged path. When they reached something of a shelf in the cliff side, just before highest ground began, The Soul Collector ordered his men to stay low and boldly walked forward on what was something of a trail cut through the tall grasses. Damián crawled on all fours towards two large rocks, where from behind, he could view the land ahead but remain camouflaged from prying eyes.

The Soul Collector was surprisingly stealthy when traveling on sand. He could move somewhat swiftly when it served his purpose, and when he heard the unmistakable wail of a woman's cry, he withdrew his pole arm and began moving toward it more rapidly. As he moved further along the trail, the grasses seemed to grow shorter, and a clearing came into view just ahead of him.

Night was taking over, but the sky above remained largely free of clouds. Seemingly one by one, a star pierced the veil of darkness with flittering strands of light, and the moon was just beginning to rise into view.

The Soul Collector's night vision was excellent. He could clearly make out several trees on the edges of the clearing beyond. He ceased his movement when he heard the clamoring cries of bats once again. So he stood still and listened intently to the sounds of the night air.

The woman's voice shrieked out again in terror. Then he saw the shape of a white dress, almost pure and blinding under the light of the stars, and it was moving toward him rather quickly.

"Help me!" she cried as she stumbled forward. With every footstep closer she sobbed in pain and in panic. The Soul Collector sensed a woman as terrified as any he had ever come across in all his long years. And yet, she ran towards... *him*.

The Soul Collector scanned around with his eyes and then carefully approached her. He could hear the whispers of sinister voices echoing in the darkness. The closer he got to the clearing, the more easily he could see his surroundings.

He found stones positioned in an unusual manner, not unlike an arrangement he had seen somewhere in his travels before. There were movements around the stones, and shadows that had no explanation.

The woman stopped cold on the path just ahead of him, by about fifteen feet. Her dress was so beautiful and bright from a distance, but up close, he could see it was dirty, tattered, and ripped repeatedly along the bottom hem. Blood stains dripped down from the left of her neck line and over her breast. Yet the quality of the cloth, the extravagant use of lace and small pearls, the painstaking attention to detail, it was obviously a wedding gown.

"Please... Knight... sir," she began to say, but then broke down into tears before she could finish.

"Please sir, kill me, before I become one of them! They..." As she spoke, her fists clenched the air, as if to grasp the words she so desperately sought to speak.

"They ravaged me. I carry the seed of one of them... *inside me*. I have been bitten. I am becoming just like them. Please sir, by whatever name you go by, and by whatever you hold dear in this world, please kill me!"

The young woman then suddenly sprinted towards The Soul Collector. He held his pole arm at the ready. When it was clear she intended to run it through herself, he tucked it away, behind his back, and she threw herself into his chest and grabbed him with all her strength.

"Please!" she began to beg him again. "Please kill me, and this demon spawn I will soon carry. It is not murder if you do! I am already as good as dead. I do not want to walk the earth as some repulsive abomination, as their slave!"

The woman looked up at him. She was quite young, nineteen at the most, gorgeous, with shining flaxen curls and kind eyes. He noticed that one eye was green while the other was changing to a sky blue color, just as the strigoi literature described. The Soul Collector gently lifted a handful of her hair, and he could see that down near the roots, the color of strawberry was beginning to take hold.

He knew he was witnessing the very transformation he had read about only a few hours before. He presumed she was stolen from her groom to be on the eve of her wedding, and then taken to the place and time they now shared. In a rare moment of genuine consideration, he pitied her. At the same time, he was totally stunned by her actions toward him.

For all his time in the continuum, men and women fled his presence, and yet this young woman, barely more than a girl, ran right into his arms. All she could see in the darkness was a towering human form and the silhouette of his great helm. To her, in the twilight of her very humanity, he was a knight, a god send, someone sent to relieve her from an eternity of horrors.

To him, she was just a girl, one he was not prepared to encounter, and one he was unsure he would regret crossing paths with. She was a surprising addition to his field trip, his experiment, as it were. If not for his pity, and the urgency of his mission, he would have pulled up a log and simply watched the transformation unfold, from innocent bride to blood sucking vampire. The Soul Collector turned the blade of his pole arm towards the ground and drove it deep into the soil. He practically had to peel the weeping girl's arms from his waist.

"I am not a knight," he said at last. His voice was plain, and coldly matter of fact, as it most always was. "I came to see the one in charge," he added.

"No!" she cried out. "They will kill you! I can see that you are very large, and you must be some kind of warrior with that armor and your spear. I am sure you are brave and strong for your country, but these... *things*... they will kill you, if you are lucky. If not, you will become one of them." The Soul Collector slowly, but firmly, placed his gloved hand over her mouth.

"Highly unlikely," he plainly stated in return. The young girl pulled his hand away from her face.

"The males. They are strong. Your spear, it won't hurt them," she added, just as The Soul Collector turned away. He was becoming annoyed by her insistence on speaking. "Please, before you go, do it, before it is too late." As she implored him, she also moved in front of him to block his path. The Soul Collector could hardly believe the nature of the conversation, and quickly surmised what his next steps were to be.

"If they cannot or will not restore you to your former state of being, I will end your torment before it is too late. On this, you have my word," he offered, while struggling to achieve a note that bordered on decency.

The young girl nodded, and moved in close behind his wavering cape as The Soul Collector began walking the path toward the clearing once more.

"My name is Darla," she offered, to which there would be no reply. "If you are not a knight, then what are you?" she asked, examining the strange markings that adorned his armor. The Soul Collector, for reasons totally unclear to him, had to fight the urge to reply in succinct honesty.

"Think of me as a diplomat," he responded. The young girl didn't quite know what to make of his answer.

"Tell me," he began, "when you were bitten, did you continue to bleed from the wound in your neck afterward?" he asked.

"For a while, yes, but my heart grows faint. It barely beats now and my skin is cold. I don't even know how it is that I am walking on my two feet. I must be turning into, you know, one of the undead." The Soul Collector halted briefly, and then turned to face her.

He said nothing. He placed his gloved hand on her chest, and then gently around her neck. He could barely feel her pulse, but it was there. He could see her ribs expanding and contracting. In this moment, she was probably the only human in the entire world's history that was ever actually comforted by his normally icy touch. She felt none of the cold effects his presence had on typical human beings, which only added to his intrigue regarding her condition.

"You are still breathing. You are alive," he said, then abruptly pulled his hand away and began walking ahead again. After another thirty paces or so, he stopped.

He suddenly remembered where he had seen a similar collection of stones during his travels long ago. He had seen them on the isle of Malta, and in Wiltshire, England. The resemblance to what is known in modern times as Stonehenge was fantastic, and striking in similarity.

The giant rocks seemed to glow with some unnatural power aided only by the moon and star light. The Soul Collector wondered if they acted as a beacon for the bats when they returned to the island at night.

The moon had crept high in the sky, and for The Soul Collector's part, it hardly seemed like night at all. He couldn't remember seeing so many stars all at once. To him, the light was useful in that hour, but a perversion of what real night was supposed to be.

As they stood in the center of the upright stone arrangement, the silence was suddenly broken by the sound of a dozen or more feet all closing in from several directions. He heard broken words mixed with growls, and saw the shadows of nearly invisible figures racing toward the center of the clearing. The Soul Collector twirled his massive pole arm in a violent display of power, shifting his feet and his vision. Then the young girl cried out in pain once more.

The Soul Collector quickly scanned over her. He saw a trickle of blood running from up her dress and down to her ankle. She was also holding her hand over her mouth.

"Look, look what I've done. I have bit myself."

As he looked at her face, he found blood was slowly seeping from her lower lip. Her canine teeth were like arrowheads, and appeared to be getting longer.

"Please! You promised!" she added. The towering form said nothing. Suddenly, as if swept there by the silent wind, or materializing out of thin air, the entire strigoi colony, dozens of them, appeared all at once.

Each member of the clan was standing high up on one of the rocks in the formation. The females shrieked in laughter at the sight, while the men cackled and growled in a form of language The Soul Collector did not readily understand. He looked over the males, and tried to ascertain which one was the apex member of the colony.

They were exactly as the literature had described. Their hair was a deep and lustrous red. Their skin appeared ashen, milky, and their eyes were a haunting shade of ocean blue. Their ages ranged from what seemed to be late teens all the way into the early forties for some of the males. Finally, one of the younger men spoke out from his perch.

"You there. You must be lacking both fear and wisdom if you dare trespass here." The voice sounded incredibly parched and was of medium pitch.

"Return this woman, Darla, to her natural state and we can get down to the order of my business here." The Soul Collector's voice resonated with a dominance and authority the strigoi were completely unaccustomed to.

"Too late," growled the male strigoi. "And we care not for your business," he added.

The Soul Collector turned to face the girl. By this point, her hair had fully changed into the same deep shade of red as the others, both of her eyes were the same haunting blue. And when she stared back at him, the kindness and recognition in her gaze was almost lost.

"I know what his business is," said Darla. Her voice was beginning to turn dry and raspy like the strigoi. "He is here to set you all free. He is mercy. He is the power of eternal sleep. I know his real name. I see him now for that which he really is."

The Soul Collector could not believe his auditory senses. Darla could, in fact, see him clearly for what he was. She was in a place no human before had been in his presence. She was drifting between states of the continuum, and from there, she could see right through The Soul Collector's helm and armor and state his actual name if she chose to expose him.

But in one barely lingering moment, the kindness returned to her young eyes. She wore no intent to betray him in her expression. She smiled, ever so subtly at him.

"You promised," she begged softly, and with the natural voice she was born with.

She slowly closed her eyes, pointed her face to the sky, and exhaled audibly so that he would hear it. Without a second of hesitation, The Soul Collector swung his pole arm in a blinding flash of silver.

The cut was quick and clean. Her head tumbled backward and out of sight, while her body dropped to its knees and remained upright for a few seconds. The headless torso briefly reached out with both arms and embraced the air just before falling forward to the ground. The blood that oozed forth from her severed neck was extremely dark, almost entirely absent any red, and unnaturally thick.

The entire strigoi colony, acting perfectly as one, bared their teeth and garishly roared their rage. Their collective voice echoed across the clearing and deep into the unknown land beyond. The young male strigoi, the only one to have articulated any words to that point, leapt down from his perch. He then leapt again without taking a single step, and hurled himself at the towering figure.

So great was his speed, it appeared he was actually flying. The Soul Collector's reaction was just a split second too slow. His hewing blade hissed through the air, but the strigoi flew in under the stroke, and rammed The Soul Collector's body clean from his feet. His pole arm went twirling to the side as the two struck the ground with thunderous force.

The Soul Collector's massive arms had no problem pushing the relatively small strigoi off of his chest, but the young creature was unrelenting as he clawed at his armor and helm.

"She was mine!" the young strigoi howled. His clawed hands moved with the speed of a panther's paws as they tried, in vain, to inflict damage on his much larger opponent's body. "You had no right to take her from me! She was to be my bride for eternity!"

When the young strigoi's hands grasped a hold of the bottom of The Soul Collector's helm, it moved just slightly, and nearly broke free from the rigid collar that held it in place. The Soul Collector then used his advantage in size and heft to roll them both over.

Once on top, he quickly subdued the strigoi's hands, and began smashing the brow of his great helm into the strigoi's face repeatedly. The first blow crushed the strigoi's nose in a revolting splatter of blood and mutilated bone. The second knocked most of his front teeth out, save for the pronounced canines. The third and forth blows shattered each of the strigoi's orbital bones, splitting the flesh deeply both times, and blackening its skin almost instantaneously.

The Soul Collector rose to his feet smoothly as he held the strigoi's shirt in his hand. Once upright, the strigoi was no longer under his own power. The Soul Collector punched him in the stomach so hard, it lifted the strigoi's feet off the ground by almost a foot. He then kicked the strigoi in the crotch with his spiked boot. The blow sounded like it almost cracked the strigoi's pelvis in half.

The Soul Collector then picked up the strigoi like a log, with both hands, and hurled him into one of the upright stones. The young strigoi's skull struck with such force, the stone facade cracked and spilled a collection of rock fragments on his limp body as it landed. The remaining strigoi, perched on the rocks above, all snarled in disapproval, and began yelling for their brother to fight back.

"Come on!" a voice called out from the shadows. "You are a shame to the colony if you let this man beat you! Get up! Kill him!" cried a second voice.

The Soul Collector could feel their anger swelling, like rising floodwaters about to burst right through the dam that contained them. So he toed his pole arm into the air with his right foot and prepared to hack at anything that came near him. His eyes then flashed a menacing yellow warning that made the massive stones all about them glow even brighter in the moonlit night.

The composite anger of the strigoi colony seemed to wane as a result, but much to The Soul Collector's surprise, it was not the yellow glow from under his helm that was responsible. The young strigoi he had thrown head first into a stone pillar was already back on his feet.

The strigoi's face was mangled beyond recognition, but there he stood, with blood almost black in color oozing from the assorted injuries to his head. The young strigoi leapt at The Soul Collector again, covering some twenty feet in the air in a single bound. But this time, The Soul Collector's pole arm pierced the strigoi in the stomach, and impaled him so deep, the blade ran right through his back and the parrying hooks submerged inside of his flesh.

The Soul Collector held the strigoi aloft where it could get no leverage against the pole arm at all. The strigoi at first tried to push himself free of the blade. When that didn't work, he tried to pull it all the way through. But the parrying hooks were embedded in such a way the raging strigoi couldn't extract the blade in either direction. So he flailed wildly with all his limbs in a hopeless display of anger and fury. The remaining strigoi, all of them accustomed to having their way with whatever living creature they encountered, seemed paralyzed with indecision.

"I like your spirit," The Soul Collector said at last.

Upon hearing these words, the impaled strigoi ceased struggling, and the members of his colony became silent. The Soul Collector took a few steps forward, and continued to hold the creature aloft. He carried him to where his feet dangled just above a stone table that was stained with blood. It looked conspicuously like a place that had been used for human sacrifice. The Soul Collector was so strong, he had no problem holding the spear and the strigoi aloft with one hand.

With his free hand now open, the blue orb of energy suddenly appeared from his palm and illuminated the entire landscape. When the gateway to The Soul Collector's spiritual prison opened, and the blue light burned into the strigoi's eyes, the reaction was unlike any he had seen before.

The strigoi began to struggle violently as his life force and the remains of his demented soul began to depart from his undead body. The Soul Collector found the extraction unusually difficult. So he spread his fingers apart, widening the orb and intensifying the power of the gateway that he alone controlled.

The strigoi's body pulsated frantically while his extremities began to sizzle and burn. The scent was intense, like a pile of bloated and decaying animal corpses suddenly set ablaze by a powerful bolt of lightning. At last the strigoi's soul exited through its hollering mouth as if shot from of a cannon and vanished into the orb.

The young creature's body burst into flame. The resulting explosion showered the surrounding area with sparks and miniature pyres of fatty tissue and smoking bone fragments. The entire event only took a matter of seconds, but it seemed to drag on for minutes. As the colony of strigoi shrieked and recoiled in terror, The Soul Collector's eyes widened in a curious but satisfied astonishment.

When he lowered his pole arm, he found hardly any remains of his assailant, save for some dark, brownish-black blood that lingered in the fuller of the blade. When he turned his focus back to the table, The Soul Collector saw the strigoi's shiny black boots had fallen off its feet in the commotion. They looked to be of fine quality, probably Italian, and somehow had landed on the stone table top perfectly upright.

The air had grown still and strangely silent. The entire colony of strigoi had retreated from their stone perches and into the shadows, out of sight.

"Some nice looking boots!" The Soul Collector shouted. Smoke billowed from both the leather shafts while the remnants of the strigoi's feet still smoldered down inside of them. "Would anyone care to fill them?" he added, as he smiled devilishly behind his steel veil.

Just then, a tall, thin man who looked to be in his forties with hollow looking cheeks and lengthy maroon strands of hair stepped out from behind one of the upright stone pillars. He wore a dark and ragged looking overcoat. He also had a gold medallion, one engraved with the face of a gargoyle, which hung from his neck. The Soul Collector assumed this identified him as the apex of the colony; the one he was seeking.

"It is bad enough that you've come here and killed two of our kind. You don't need to make a mockery of it!"

The elder strigoi hissed like a snake as he spoke. Like the others, his voice sounded dry, raspy, but without the bestial snarls and bare fangs, it was proper sounding enough.

"I killed *one* of your kind. The girl was a prisoner who asked me to set her free. So I did," The Soul Collector responded.

"You had no right! The girl was to be one of us. You denied her an eternity with one of my brothers," barked the strigoi, who then slapped the smoking pair of boots off the table top and onto the ground.

"That girl was about as Romanian as I am a dwarf. Golden hair, green eyes, she was German or Dutch or... the point being, it was *you* who had *no right* to take her from where ever she lived and make her your slave." The Soul Collector found himself unusually aggravated by the conversation, and had to shake himself free of the dialogue's effects.

"I am not going to argue the point. I am Dragomir. You stated you had some business to discuss. So state your purpose and be on your way. We have our own business to attend to."

The yellow glow of the Soul Collector's eyes intensified. No one ever spoke to him in such a dismissive manner.

"Listen closely, you blood sucking parasite. By whatever name you choose, be it strigoi or vampire or incubus or whatever romantic and sophisticated sounding word, on an evolutionary scale you are nothing more than leech to me. You may be accustomed to having men fear you, but I am no man and I am not of this realm. I believe I have demonstrated my power satisfactorily. But... if you need additional examples, Dragomir, then line your kin up before me. Line them up! So I may dispatch their souls to a dungeon so remote and infernal that the stifling heat and foul stench in the deepest bowels of Hell will seem like a welcome improvement. One of your brethren has already arrived there. I have plenty of room for more!"

The Soul Collector's voice boomed through the still night air just as the blue orb reappeared in his right hand and cast the coldest shroud of hollow pale light upon everything within their view. Dragomir ducked behind the stone table, shuddering in fear.

"By what authority do you threaten me thusly?" Dragomir pleaded.

The Soul Collector did not answer immediately. He wanted to make his point as crystal clear as one could be made. So he shifted his feet and walked about in a great circle among the huge stone collocation. And everywhere he shone the chilling pale light, a strigoi scampered away into the comfort of the shadows. He was taking stock, counting their numbers, so in the event he had to wipe them out, the eradication would be absolute.

Having accounted for them all, he turned the glowing gateway back toward Dragomir.

"By the authority of Jeringas Mortifer, the deity Morbus, and the wishes of the continuum of being, I am here to offer the following pact. My king, Lord Mortifer, has made claim against every island in the Caribbean, including this one. He has pledged to let you and your kind remain here, in peace, to feed on the natives and carry on however you see fit. In exchange, you and those of your colony will lend your services to his cause without question or resistance."

Dragomir rose from behind the stone table and shielded his eyes from the blinding light.

"Mortifer? We chose this island for the very purpose of respectfully avoiding him. No settlements. No people. There is nothing here worth having. I cannot see why he would want this island, or of what service we could be to him," Dragomir replied, in a much meeker tone of voice.

"I believe you know the consequences if you refuse," The Soul Collector returned sharply. Dragomir squinted as he nodded in affirmation.

"We accept your terms and we will cooperate. You have my word. Now please, make it dark again," Dragomir softly begged.

The Soul Collector's hand then closed around the blue orb, and the light instantly vanished from view. Dragomir stumbled forward and almost fell to the ground. The exposure to the gateway's light had weakened him considerably.

"Tell me your purpose and the will of the king. We will do as you both ask," added Dragomir. His voice was laden with both exhaustion and defeat.

"I am tracking a shaman, one who is elusive and well guarded. He has been known to frequent many, if not all of the European settlements. He has something in his possession that belongs to our king. I need one of your kind to accompany me on the mission to find him. Preferably a male, one who can blend in with the European settlers and infiltrate their towns without drawing attention. The time may come when Lord Mortifer calls upon all of your kind to aid him. But for now, just the one will do." As The Soul Collector spoke, his eyes scanned about the rocky monuments, examining the strigoi as they slowly crept back towards their leader.

"I have the perfect candidate. Grul, step forward and be made known!" Dragomir called aloud.

The strigoi known as Grul swung down from a tree branch, and raced over to his leader's side. He appeared to be in his late twenties, a little under six feet tall, lean, and fit. He wore the clothes of a commoner, and was rather plain looking in his general appearance. There was nothing notable about any of his facial features. With the exception of his pale skin and haunting blue eyes, he appeared, for the most part, normal.

"This is Grul. He has already been to some of the settlements you speak of and drawn nary an unwanted glance. He is quite adept at tracking prey and handy with a sword too. I should think he would be rather useful on your man hunt." At the conclusion of Dragomir's introduction, Grul bowed before The Soul Collector.

"You have my absolute allegiance, sire. I am at your command. How should I address thee, my lord?" Grul's voice was dry and rough, but soft spoken enough not to draw suspicion among most Europeans.

"As sire, master, or your lordship for now," The Soul Collector answered, in a tone that indicated he could hardly care on the matter any less.

"You understand the duty you have been charged with?" The Soul Collector demanded. Grul nodded eagerly to the inquiry.

"Good. Should you desert on me or my company, I will return here and leave no evidence of your kin but a smoking pile of footwear. If you fulfill your duty to my satisfaction, you will be free to come back or go as you please. This journey might take only days, but more likely months. There is a remote possibility it could be even longer. We travel by sea. I will do my best to accommodate your... hunger... with whatever provisions we can acquire along the way. But if you feed upon any of my men, I will make shark food of you in short order. So welcome, Grul. Come along now. This has already taken longer than needed." The Soul Collector paused just briefly as he turned toward the trail.

The towering form then walked a few paces back to where Darla's headless corpse lay on the ground.

"Dragomir, I expect the girl to receive a proper burial. See to it."

The Soul Collector returned his pole arm to the sheath along his back, and made haste back to the trail that cut across the clearing. Grul hesitated for a moment.

Dragomir then silently motioned with his hand to follow, and the younger strigoi took off down the path afterward.

As the stone monuments and the clearing disappeared in the darkness behind, Grul could smell something in the ocean breeze as it swept upward from the rocky cliff ahead.

"I smell torches. There are men up ahead," said Grul. His voice was filled with alarm as he pointed outward to the edge of the cliff. The Soul Collector could not see any of the men, but of course he knew they were there.

"My company awaits us. Your olfactory senses are impressive," The Soul Collector commented.

Just as they reached the trailhead, Damián stood up from behind his rocky waylay and joined them.

"That took longer than expected, my lord," Damián stated plainly.

"They are a tenacious bunch, a bit hesitant at first, but not entirely without reason. Damián, this is Grul. Get him whatever equipment he needs. Grul, this is Damián. In my absence, he is in charge. Abide by him at all times. Come now, we must make haste towards the Lesser Antilles."

The Soul Collector's men held their torches aloft to light the way. But with only a half hearted wave of his hand, The Soul Collector made all of the torches extinguish in an instant. Grul was duly impressed by this action, but even more intrigued by the fact that The Soul Collector's men seemed perfectly accustomed to such an incredible demonstration of power.

Damián thoroughly examined Grul as they walked, unsure of what to make of the new addition to their outfit. The young strigoi could sense curious eyes upon him. But Grul kept his own eyes pointed to the sand, and tried his best to forget his fear of water as he climbed inside the small wooden rowboat.

"To what island should I begin plotting our next course master?" Damián inquired, as he pulled the rowboat out into the softly rolling surf. The Soul Collector stared vacantly at Grul, for he did not have an immediate answer. He then turned his head up towards the heavens, and observed the brightness of the moon. The stars seemed to shine even brighter than before. There were so many, they were innumerable.

To The Soul Collector, the parallel seemed obvious. Peiman could have been anywhere by then. Only the stars could tell for certain. And no matter how The Soul Collector may have desired otherwise, the stars were not speaking to him at all.

As his eyes came back down from the heavens, his focus was drawn away from the *Unda Jaulaor* and back towards the shore. He stared for a moment into the blackness of the caves where he originally expected to find the strigoi. Then it struck him like a whip bound from steel wire. There was a reason he and his company did not venture into the caves at all. The Soul Collector turned back to Grul once again.

"Can you really take the form of a bat, at any time of your choosing?" he asked. The young strigoi nodded rapidly, and grimaced subtly as the little rowboat smacked into the side of the *Unda Jaulaor*. The Soul Collector let out a sinister yet hardly audible chortle.

"That... is *truly* outstanding!" he asserted loudly.

After the crew ascended back to the deck and hoisted the rowboats topside, Damián lit a lantern and began pouring over a chart of the Lesser Antilles. The Soul Collector walked over and folded the chart in two.

"We won't be needing that. The trail may have gone stale, but even stale crumbs are better than no bread at all. I know where we are going, and you already know the way. Deploy the main sails! I want maximum speed! Send a messenger craft to Lord Mortifer with word of our success here and our intended destination. We make for the Dragon's Mouth. I want us there in two days, Damián. Make it happen."

Though he was concerned by the order, Damián did not question it, and immediately took his position at the helm while the rest of the crew prepared the ship for travel. The Soul Collector glanced back up at the stars again.

Once more, he somehow knew that he was precisely where he was meant to be. More importantly, he knew precisely where the dark powers of the continuum intended for him to go.

CHAPTER TEN

THE FIRST SIGN

The following morning brought a gathering of dark clouds on stiff winds towards the island of Statia. Pieter suspected the storm would reach land by mid afternoon, so he and Franklin hurried to get the *Vissen* sailing just before the sun fully rose.

It was that time of year. The rainy season could be terribly unpredictable. Sometimes, the approaching storm fronts made the schools of fish incredibly active at the surface and easy to locate.

On these days, a half day's work easily brought in a full day's payload. But on other days, the storms seemed to chase the fish into the depths, well out of reach of the trolling nets, and then the *Vissen* would come home empty. Pieter wasn't sure what sort of day he had ahead of him. All he knew was if lightning began to touch down anywhere within his view, he and his first mate had better find cover somewhere on land in a hurry.

Meanwhile, back on the island, Lauren and little Stephen were enjoying some time together on the beach while Dorothy kept watch over things from the dock. Lauren rarely took him to the waterfront for any length of time. Little Stephen was too young, his skin was too easy to burn.

On this particular day, the overcast sky and cool winds afforded them both a rare opportunity to have some play time away from the house. Being just a matter of days old, little Stephen could not walk or even crawl under his own power. But he was remarkably curious, and learned the value of pointing to different things in no time.

"What's that you see there?" Lauren asked. "Is that the big wide ocean?" Little Stephen giggled and reached out with his tiny hands. "Does baby want to get wet? Huh? You want to get wet?" Lauren asked playfully.

Lauren picked the child up and sat down in the water with him where it was only a few inches deep. The sea was a perfectly warm and enjoyable temperature. Baby Stephen laughed hysterically when the remains of a small wave washed over them both.

"Your father was right. You do love all things wet," said Lauren. As the small wave receded back into the inlet, Lauren spotted a particularly colorful hermit crab crawling along in the wet sand. The crab was the color of peach, with a pronounced, bright purple claw that wonderfully contrasted the cream colored shell it called home.

Lauren had probably seen a million or more of them in her time on Statia, and she always found them to be amusing little creatures. So she picked the crab up by the shell and held it up for little Stephen to see. The crab was so big, it couldn't retract its body all the way back into its shell.

"Look at this pretty little thing, huh?" Baby Stephen pointed to the crab and then held his hands out, as if asking to inspect it.

"Oh no, little one, you don't want to handle this guy, not yet. He might be cute, but that big purple claw will pinch your tiny little fingers if you let him. It is almost August. He is probably out here looking for a girlfriend. Say bye-bye!"

As Lauren set the crab back down for the next wave to come and carry it away, little Stephen barely murmured the sound of "buh-buh," as if repeating what his mother had said.

"Oh my goodness!" Lauren proclaimed. "Did you just say bye-bye to the crab?" she inquired excitedly. Little Stephen laughed hysterically once again, and then returned to making sounds that seemed to have no rhyme or reason.

The wind started to pick up and sprayed saltwater off the crests of incoming waves. Since getting the mist into her eyes was not the most pleasant experience, Lauren picked Stephen up and took him to the foot of the dock where Dorothy was seated.

"You have been very quiet today," Lauren commented as Dorothy took the baby.

"Oh, just thinking about the men, and thinking in general. That little one of yours, he seems unusually aware of his surroundings," said Dorothy as she shifted the baby to her shoulder.

"How so?" Lauren inquired.

"It's like, the whole world is new to him, as it should be for a newborn baby. But then it's like he is comfortable with everything new in a matter of seconds. And his eyes, they are always moving, like he is looking for something. Newborns usually take time to see much in detail. I cannot tell for sure what he sees without looking through those little baby blues, but I swear, it seems he sees every moving leaf, and every cloud as it goes by. He is all curious and never afraid. He never seems to cry, which you should feel lucky for. But I feel sorry for you when he gets to crawling around and then to standing. He is going to be into everything."

Lauren chuckled as she rung the water out of the bottom of her light summer dress in the wind.

"Oh, you are just jealous of how smart and well behaved my little man is," Lauren said sarcastically.

"He has so much of your big man in him. He is smart. He is well behaved. For now," said Dorothy, as she flashed a humorously sadistic smile at Lauren.

"This storm looks like it is going to be a bad one. We had better go make sure the awnings are drawn down or else our homes will be soaked. I don't like the *Vissen* being absent at this hour. They should be coming in ahead of that storm," added Dorothy, just as she handed the baby back to Lauren.

"Pieter is probably on a good school of fish and, knowing him, running circles around them to get the biggest catch he can. Pieter will get them home. He always does," Lauren assured her friend.

Dorothy looked at Stephen and then into the trees just beyond the sand dunes behind them. She repeated this several times before letting her eyes settle on one of the tree tops.

"Dorothy?" Lauren asked.

"I swear he sees something. He won't keep his eyes off that mango tree next to the trailhead," Dorothy replied, as she scanned the tree top herself. Lauren paused to look up as well.

"There is some ripening fruit up there, a couple red sides, and not much else. Maybe he sees the fruit. Come on, we need to head in," said Lauren. As she kissed little Stephen on the cheek, whatever held his attention in the trees suddenly lost its grip. He made a splattering sound with his lips and began to giggle again.

"See Dorothy? Nothing to it. Let's go."

Lauren walked on ahead while Dorothy followed slowly with her eyes turned up toward the tree tops. As they passed underneath the mango tree, Dorothy stopped and looked up under the tree's canopy. When she still failed to see anything of interest, she hurried along to catch up with Lauren. But then she heard a rustling from above that couldn't have possibly been made by the wind. As Lauren reached the porch of her home, a very large broad winged hawk flew out from the mango tree. It went blazing across the village square and landed on the roof of Lauren and Pieter's house.

"Lauren! Did you see that?" Dorothy exclaimed. Just as Dorothy ran across the village square, a light drizzle began to fall.

"See what?" Lauren cried back. The broad winged hawk walked along the roof's center ridge toward the rear of the house, until it was completely out of view. Dorothy cupped one hand over her eyes to keep the rain from getting in them, and then scampered off the wet lawn to the porch.

"It was a hawk! There was a hawk up in that mango tree and it is walking around on your roof right now. That must have been what Stephen was staring at. It is huge!" Dorothy said excitedly.

"A hawk? Are you sure? I have not seen one of those in years," Lauren responded thoughtfully.

"There was no mistaking it, Lauren. It was big and beautiful. I swear, your son knew it was in that tree when we were on the beach. Now it is up there, somewhere on your roof."

Lauren wanted to step out for a peek but she didn't want to get herself or little Stephen soaked in the rain.

"I will take your word on it. I am not sure if that is a good omen. Hawks usually feed on mice or rats. I hope we don't have any of them moving in," Lauren commented. Dorothy shrugged her shoulders with a smile, and then rushed home to tend to her windows. Lauren went inside and did the same before she took Stephen into the bedroom and prepped him for a nap.

Roughly 150 miles southeast of Statia, on the island of Aichi, The Seer of the Sister Islands was deep in meditation, hidden away in the spare bedroom of a friend's house. She had vacated her sacellum for the time being.

While this did not sit well with clients seeking her guidance, the other members of her order stood in for her and gave readings in The Seer's stead at a discount. This was all under the guise that The Seer had become ill, and was traveling abroad in the search of treatment.

The house she was staying in belonged to her friend Nerea, who was also a junior member of the order. Nerea was only around twenty five years of age, short, and voluptuously shaped.

She was a full blooded Carib, with medium length, silky dark hair and eyes, and a tan so perfectly golden brown she looked like she stepped out of an oil painting. Much like The Seer, she wore loose fitting, inconspicuous tan clothing, and very little jewelry. Much like The Seer, she did not need anything else to draw the attention of men.

When Nerea knocked at the door, it opened just slightly on its own. Nerea stepped inside with a tray of freshly prepared fruit and a pitcher of water. When she looked upon The Seer of the Sister islands, she saw sweat running from her hairline down her face and neck. The Seer was rocking on the floor in a soft rhythm, almost like a series of convulsions that had slowed to a crawl.

"Yoana?" Nerea asked, softly. Rarely did she address The Seer by her first name alone. "Yoana, are you all right?" Nerea inquired again. At last, The Seer broke free of the trance that held her, and looked up at Nerea. Yoana's face broadcast a depiction of chilling fear.

"Yoana! I thought you came here to hide out. I thought you were going to avoid use of the third eye so long as Azura might be using it too." Nerea's voice came heavy with dread, because whatever Yoana was hiding from, Nerea did not want The Seer inadvertently leading it to them both.

"I have learned how to know when Azura is looking. In time, we may be able to use that to our gain. Today, the continuum called upon me, so I had to look. I was once mildly concerned that the black king would send forth his soldiers and spies to look for Pieter's child. My concern was mild because they are just mindless proxies compared to the events of the lost prophecy unfolding. But then I felt something altogether new. It was like the entire continuum was shaken, even the Hallowed Guardians of light trembled from up above. It is because of the one Mortifer unleashed, the faceless death, the one the Spaniards call *El Ladrón De Almas*."

The Seer's wet hair clung to her neck and face as she took the pitcher of water and nearly consumed it whole.

"You saw him?" Nerea asked. The Seer nodded in such a way, the answer was without question.

"I saw him as clearly as if he were standing next to you now. I get the strange feeling that the light powers of the continuum might possibly fear him even more than Lord Mortifer himself. It feels like the thief of spirits came from a place he was never meant to escape, as though neither side intended for him to be of this realm again. But he is here. He is coming this way." The Seer of the Sister Islands quietly nibbled at a piece of fruit, and tried to regain her composure.

"So it is true. Everything the Spaniards said, it is true. The terrible thief of souls really is among us. Where is he headed?" As Nerea inquired, the bowls and silverware on the tray within her hands began to rattle.

"I am uncertain. But do not worry, he is not coming for me, not yet. I do not think he is even aware that I exist. I do not understand how I have come to know this, because the vision did not foretell of his path, but I get the sense *El Ladrón* is seeking the wise man, Peiman. He must be warned. He must know that his is life is in danger, as are the lives of anyone within his company. Peiman can be stubborn at times, not easily swayed by the threat of danger. I must reach him first." As she finished speaking, Yoana's eyes welled with tears.

"What is the matter?" asked Nerea.

"I yearn to see Pieter. He must be warned too. But I fear if I see him again so soon, I will love him," The Seer replied somberly.

"Pieter is a married man. And I think you already have gotten too close to him. Send me instead. I will not draw attention. If you go and are seen, you might lead Mortifer's people right to the Child of Prophecy. Peiman is on the island of Camahogne, further south. He is well protected there. You would be too if you joined him," Nerea plainly stated.

"Yoana, what is this being, *El Ladrón De Almas*? What is he, and can he be stopped?" The Seer let out a small but desperate laugh at the inquiry.

"I do not know. Only Peiman can say for sure. This is why I must see him. I cannot risk you. I will not send you over the seas to find Pieter. You cannot know where he lives. I cannot risk it if you were caught, neither can Pieter, or his son. Something is about to happen. I can feel it, Nerea. Something will send Pieter in my direction. He will arrive at the sacellum in a day's time. I will ask that you be there when he comes. There is something else though. Something else is coming. I had a vision of a dark tide coming in. It was almost black. I do not know what it means. Nerea, you must be on guard, and be wary of strangers, especially if they arrive at the sacellum first, before Pieter." Nerea quietly nodded in understanding.

"For now, the ocean is too angry to travel. I will head for the harbor, and make haste for Camahogne the moment this storm has broken." The Seer had made up her mind, and Nerea was not about to attempt changing it.

"I will do as you ask, *Madre de la Tercero Ojo*. I will wait for Pieter at the Sacellum, all night if it pleases you, and I will be vigilant in your absence. For now, you must eat. Gather your strength. You have a long way to travel. I will not let you leave on an empty stomach."

Nerea offered the plate of cut fruit to Yoana. Together they quietly nibbled at their food and watched as huge sheets of rain came rolling across the bright green pastures outside.

Meanwhile, sitting alone in the highest lookout tower that protruded from his fortress, Jeringas Mortifer stared out across the hilltops and the valleys. He was watching the twelve mile road back to Catia La Mar. He waited for a mounted rider to suddenly appear behind the veil of gray rainfall.

He expected one of The Soul Collector's messengers to make land at some time within the next day or two. He just wasn't entirely sure when. He had great faith in his chief lieutenant, and suspected the first leg of Angelis' journey was successful. He too, felt the quake, the tremble, the energetic quiver of the entire continuum as it shifted, and Jeringas Mortifer just knew The Soul Collector's enterprise was directly at the heart of all the motions in play. Beneath his veil, he smiled contently at the thought.

Across the seas, the master of the *Unda Jaulaor*, The Soul Collector himself, had his arm wrapped around the center mast of his ship. He was facing forward, scanning outward, and trying to decide whether the remains of his squadron should alter their course.

He had ordered Damián to reach the Dragon's Mouth in two days time, and while it appeared they were on the quickest nautical course, their current heading was one that was about to take them into a potent storm that evidently spanned out for miles.

His practical nature would tell him to simply go around it. They would probably gain time in this case, because the winds did not favor an eastward passage. But his instinct told him something entirely different.

209

Something about this storm seems to be... unnatural, he thought to himself.

"My lord, if we cut south now, we can catch the spiral edge of the system and gain speed on our sails. But if we don't do it soon, we're going to be in for a long night!" Damián cried from the helm. "What are your orders, my lord?"

The Soul Collector could feel the gathering sea beneath the hull rising further and further. He stared ahead, seeking outward with his thoughts, seeking, staring, combing through the waves and the winds with the vision of his mind as if it were some astral form of sonar.

"Your orders, my lord?" Damián called once again, with his voice escalating in its urgency.

Meanwhile, on board the *Vissen,* Captain Pieter Thomas and his first mate Franklin were busy with trying to stave off a total disaster. The seas were high and rolling. The winds were stiff and blowing westward, away from their home. The day had been fortunate early on, as the two men harvested a huge catch. But with Pieter's penchant for keeping fish alive, which meant keeping them in a pen on board full of water, the *Vissen* was unusually sluggish and unresponsive on the return journey. Had the cargo bay been empty, they might have outrun the storm entirely. But even though the *Vissen's* hull hung low and heavy in the water, and wave after wave pounded the deck with impunity, Pieter was determined to keep his haul.

While the captain and his first mate struggled to gain distance over the rolling seas and against the wind, a much larger and more seaworthy vessel was closing in from behind. The two men were getting soaked, and their bodies were running low on strength.

Franklin hauled the lines and played the canvas. Pieter held fast to the wheel of his ship as the grappling currents tossed them in every direction. Neither of them were aware of the black sailed ship that loomed against the western skyline; that the *Unda Jaulaor* and The Soul Collector were on a heading that could overtake the *Vissen* well before the fall of night.

Pieter could hardly hear a thing above the howling winds, the whipping of the sails as they blew about, and the smashing of the wooden hull as it climbed over a wave and rolled downward into the next. But he heard an echoing reminder of the ghostly deep voice that had haunted him in his dreams just two days before.

Patris... he heard it call, deep within his mind. He knew the sound did not come from Franklin. His first mate was too far away, in the stern of the ship. No, he knew it to be within his mind alone. Pieter wondered whether it was just a trick of the brain, perhaps a warning from his own subconscious, that it was time for him to be home with his child.

So he shrugged it off, he gave it no reply, not even with the silent words in his own mind. The captain fought on with newfound focus and strength, though the sky ahead showed no mercy was gathering on its darkened horizon.

Back on Statia, the slight drizzle had become a torrential downpour over the island. Lauren had expected Dorothy to return, so they would at least have each other's company while waiting for their husbands to return. After changing the baby and herself, little Stephen pointed to the bookshelf against the wall. It was clear he was pointing to an empty sea shell.

"You recognize this, do you?" Lauren happily asked. Baby Stephen made some adorable little noise and clapped his hands.

"It looks just like the one you saw on the beach today, right? Except this one has been on the shelf for a very long time. No pinching claws are going come out of this one to get you!" Lauren exclaimed.

Little Stephen smiled bright and cheerfully at the sight of his mother reaching to pick up the shell. Lauren put it up to his ear for a moment.

"Can you hear the ocean in there?" She asked. Little Stephen seemed to concentrate for a moment, and then laughed hysterically at what he was hearing.

"Here, you can take it. This one cannot hurt you," Lauren added, and gently placed the shell in Stephen's little hands.

Baby Stephen fumbled with the shell for a moment. He held it close to his eyes, as if he was looking for the crab inside. Then he shook it around, half expecting something to come out. Lauren's face lit up like a star on a moonless night, for she loved seeing how the whole universe was new and fascinating again through the eyes and ears and fingers of her baby.

But then for a moment, Stephen became quiet, almost serious, as if an infant could be as such. And then, for no apparent reason, he smiled and laughed uncontrollably again while offering the shell back to his mother.

"Should I put it back? All done?" Lauren asked.

As Stephen placed the shell back into her hands, she felt something poke out of the shell and into her palm that startled her. When she turned it over, she saw the unmistakable beady eyes of a hermit crab and a purple claw tucked down inside. Her hands immediately flew apart as the shell dropped down onto the bed.

Little Stephen just sat there giggling. He pointed at the shell, as if he had just played the world's greatest joke on his mother. Lauren laughed briefly, but with fear shaking in her voice.

"You think that was funny, little man?" she asked, as the hermit crab began crawling across the bed. Lauren was absolutely stunned, unsure what to make of what she had just seen. She watched silently as the crab casually crawled across the bed, and then tumbled off the other edge.

"How did that just happen?" she whispered to no one but herself.

Little Stephen clapped his hands and then went about the business of inspecting a wrinkle in the bed's comforter. Lauren walked around the other side of the bed to where the crab fell. It was still moving towards the wall.

So she picked it up and tossed it out the window where it landed harmlessly in the yard. Baby Stephen was totally oblivious to his mother's stare, or her thoughts. Just as suddenly as it came, the storm outside relented. Emergent strands of blue sky began to ward off the menacing clouds that encompassed the island just minutes before.

Within the hour, the front door slowly swung open, and Pieter came walking in. He was dripping from head to toe, exhausted, but feeling rather victorious. The *Vissen* had survived the storm, and was safely tied down dockside for the remains of the day.

The men retained their hefty catch after carefully considering whether to jettison it all at once. Pieter wanted nothing more than a hot cup of tea and some dry clothes. But before he could even change his shirt, Lauren ran right into him, and squeezed him with all her might.

"My lord, look at you!" she burst out. "I thought you were lost or shipwrecked or worse. I am so happy you are home now."

Pieter was about to explain his late arrival, or perhaps brag about his catch, and how he and Franklin only narrowly avoided sinking from taking on too much water. But Lauren began rambling uncontrollably about the events with Stephen and the sea shell. Pieter was so tired, he could hardly understand a word at first. Eventually she settled down, and Pieter began to follow what she was saying.

"You are certain this was the same shell that was on the shelf?" Pieter asked. Lauren nodded repeatedly, and with no hesitation.

"I mean, could a crab in the surf have caught onto his diaper while you were both playing, and hitched a ride on him all the way into the house? Maybe you didn't notice it until it fell on the bed?"

Lauren grabbed Pieter by the arm and hastily led him to the bedroom. She pointed to the shelf where the cream colored shell was now missing.

"Pieter, I know what I saw. Go look in the yard!" she exclaimed, and rushed to the window. "There, there it is now. It is right there. Go pick up that shell and see for yourself if you do not believe me."

Pieter slowly stepped over to the window and looked outside. It was still light enough to see, and he was able to spot the shell quickly.

"Lauren, dear, please bring me some dry clothes," he requested kindly.

When Lauren left the room to do as he asked, Pieter looked down at little Stephen for a moment. He was sound asleep. Pieter began to remove his soaking wet shirt and pants, while never once taking his eye off the shell laying in the grass. Even when Lauren returned, and helped him into his fresh attire, Pieter still stared blankly at the shell.

"Maybe you were seeing things," he said at last. "I have watched that shell all this time and it has not budged. Maybe you are tired and stressed. We just had a baby after all. I have seen some unusual things these last few days myself. I have heard a few unusual... sounds... as well. The mind can do funny things when you are tired," Pieter offered with a half hearted smile.

Lauren held her index finger upward, and shook it. "I am not crazy. Get it. You'll see," she responded.

Pieter sighed and walked to the door. Lauren stayed in the room and watched as Pieter retrieved the shell. When he picked it up and began walking around to the front door, Lauren met him on the porch.

"I don't want you to bring it inside. Now look!" she demanded.

Pieter turned the shell over in his hand and looked inside. He unknowingly rolled his eyes when he saw there was no crab anywhere inside of it. He even stuck his pinky finger inside the shell and then held it aloft. He waggled the shell back and forth as it was stuck to his finger with the same half hearted smile growing again on his face.

"It is empty. You can put it back on the shelf where it was," he said.

Lauren's eyes grew wide and confused. She reached over, took the shell from his hands and inspected it thoroughly. Seeing nothing, she placed the shell on the porch, grabbed one of Pieter's work boots, and then smashed the shell open with the heel.

There was nothing inside.

"I am not crazy," she reiterated.

"No one said that you are. And I do not think that you are. You have had a rough day. But I know I have had one hell of a day, and I have to get off of these feet. My legs are like limp boot straps. My arms are just dead weight. Come lay with me for a while. Then, I will get up and make us some dinner." As Pieter spoke, he gently put his arm around his wife, and led her back into the house.

Lauren laid back on the bed first, while Pieter stood before Stephen's crib and smiled. When he laid down next to his wife, his body finally at rest, he heard something from Lauren so unexpected, he thought for sure he was dreaming.

"Pieter, I know he is your son. He is my son too, and I love him, more than words can tell. But even aside from this matter today, there are times when, Pieter, this child… he frightens me." Pieter's eyes slowly crept back open, and he could see in Lauren's face that her words were genuine.

What? Pieter privately asked himself. He dared not ask the question aloud.

The *Unda Jaulaor* was quietly sailing south as the sun began to set. The Soul Collector had decided in the last possible moment to turn away from the storm, unwilling to chase a hunch in the interests of time. He sat alone on the bow of his great ship, scanning the seas ahead of them, questioning whether the right decision had been made.

He estimated his ship's heading would have taken them to San Kitts or Nevis had they fought through the storm to continue on. Damián was right about the danger, however. Their lead scouting craft had gotten separated from the group and then vanished, lost to the angry swells. With only two boats left in the squadron, the risk was too great for them to continue.

Damián was also correct about the winds. They were gathering speed on their heading south, well on pace to make the Dragon's Mouth in under 48 hours. The Soul Collector made a note to himself regarding the area where the scouting craft was lost. It happened at the same time he felt his strange apprehension somewhere ahead within the storm. He planned to return there as quickly as he could arrange to. The Soul Collector then turned his focus back towards Peiman and the task at hand. For the time being, he would consider his misgivings no further.

As Pieter and Lauren drifted off together, the broad winged hawk swooped down off of their roof and into the yard. The hawk began to slowly walk toward the path that led through the village square and down to the beach. Not that anyone was looking, but it was a peculiar sight to see, a hawk, tip toeing down the trail.

When it reached the point where the grass turned mostly to sand, the hawk could make out barely discernible footprints, perhaps no more than a quarter inch each. Upon finding the small prints in the sand, the hawk began hopping forward, stopping every so often to look around, rapidly moving its head and eyes as birds of prey are known to do.

At last it reached the trailhead. Its eyes continued to follow the little prints in the sand. And there, beneath the setting sun, as the ocean and the waves upon it were sprinkled with gold and crimson light, the hawk could just barely make out the shape of a hermit crab that had abandoned its shell.

The sand was turning completely to pink, a reflection of the sky above, as the little crab made its way toward the water. The hawk cried aloud, then briefly took to flight, and landed just ahead of the crab.

The crab stood still for a moment, and then continued on its way toward the water. It cared for nothing, not even the hawk obstructing its path. The bird of prey intently eyed the prone hermit crab, for without a shell, it was totally defenseless. If the hawk had lips, it probably would have licked them. But then the eyes of the hawk and the crab met just briefly. Suddenly, the hungry bird had second thoughts.

The hawk cried once more, then stepped aside while the hermit crab crawled right on past, never stopping, never hesitating, all the way into the sea.

CHAPTER ELEVEN

CIMMERIAN RISING

At last light, Yoana and her company departed the island of Aichi just as the storm waned. She knew her voyage south to Camahogne would take her company right through the night and past sunrise. She was confident in her shipmates, but the long narrow dugout offered little in the way of comfort. Even with a generous spread of blankets, she did not expect sleep to come easy.

Luckily the seas were calm. The small single mast craft sliced right through what little chop was present. As The Seer of the Sister Islands began to nod off, she also began to think of Pieter, and the vision that foretold of his pending visit to the sacellum.

I hope I have made the right decision, she privately wondered. *I assured him I would be there when he sought me. Nerea is more than capable. I pray he trusts her, and accepts her council in my stead.*

The Seer listened to the sounds of the calm sea. For a moment, she thought she might have heard something from across the water. She tried to listen more closely, but it did not help her to pinpoint whatever it may have been. She was tired, and the emptiness of the great wide sea was so serene, she eventually drifted completely away from the conscious world.

A little over one hundred miles behind her, the *Unda Jaulaor* was speeding along with full sails deployed, and on virtually the same southbound heading. The Soul Collector sat in the forward bow of his ship, with his own focus facing forward, his own curiosity deeply submerged in the dark waters ahead. Like The Seer, he was unsure of what his senses were relaying.

"The crew has been rotated and is set for the night. I am going to take my leave now. I will wake before dawn," Damián announced. The Soul Collector slowly rose to his feet and scanned over the various stations of his ship.

"Very good, Damián. I would prefer you are well rested and at the helm before we travel through the Dragon's Mouth," The Soul Collector replied. Damián was slow to dismiss himself to the sleeping quarters below deck.

"You are troubled with the loss of our scouting craft. It was... an unfortunate loss. We could have used the extra boat," The Soul Collector commented. Damián stopped. He did not know whether to say anything or continue down to his hammock.

"It was only a glorified catboat, my lord. We probably should not have brought it to begin with. Small crafts like that one are easily lost to the sea. Though I did not know any of them personally, I just feel I could have done more to rescue the men who were on it." The Soul Collector walked a few paces closer until Damián turned around.

"You were under my orders. You salvaged the remainder of our squadron with your skill at the helm. Those men knew the risks in sailing too far ahead, because I specifically warned them not to. Their impatience and eagerness overwhelmed their better judgment and it cost them their lives. Understand, Damián, we did not encounter some random ordinary storm." The Soul Collector's voice was like black ice; frigid and smooth, with little variation in pitch or tone. Damián's eyebrows sprang upward.

"You mean, that storm was the result of a higher power?" The Soul Collector chuckled at the query.

"If you want to call it that. You could not have rescued those men had you attempted it. I have no doubt that storm was cast forth by the Primordial Guardians of the continuum. They did not want us to come to port anywhere near that tempest. It is something for me to consider, should the time come for us to return." Damián nodded reservedly in agreement.

"You are pondering something else," The Soul Collector added. Damián shook his head in disagreement.

"I thought you might have asked what I would do had it been you up ahead in the scout boat. It is an illogical question. You would have obeyed orders and stayed close to formation. You would have recognized the advancing storm and turned around long before endangering your crew. That is precisely why I have you in command of my own ship and men."

The Soul Collector turned and walked back to the bow in a silent dismissal. Damián took the stairs below deck. Once inside the general sleeping quarters, he climbed into his hammock, and allowed himself the tiniest smile of satisfaction over the exchange.

Meanwhile, as the hour was fast approaching the stroke of midnight, a mid sized catboat with a single, tattered black sail slowly drifted its way towards the tiny island grouping of Caaroucaëra, an archipelago that would be known in later years as Îles des Saintes, or the Islands of the Saints. Only three men of the boat's original crew of six remained. Normally tidy and wrinkle free, their black cotton uniforms were all disheveled. Their hair and bodies were dripping wet with a combination of rain and sea water.

Santha, the boat's captain, was a Carib man in his late thirties, with short dark hair, a receding hairline, and huge, bushy sideburns. His narrow brown eyes stared silently forward, hoping and watching for a place to land their boat.

Chogan was second in command, just slightly younger than his captain, with bowl cut hair and a large round face free of facial hair. He steered the boat with only one his left hand, as his other arm had been injured in the struggle to survive the squall.

Amaro was young enough to still have acne on his cheeks here and there. His long black hair was tied off in back, and he had but a small fuzzy patch of skin on his chin. Amaro was engrossed with trying to read a soaking wet map by starlight. Every lantern in the boat had either broken or become drenched with seawater, rendering it useless.

"I cannot believe we lost sight of the formation," Santha growled.

"I cannot believe they left us behind," Amaro said sheepishly. Chogan smacked Amaro across the back of the head.

"Welcome to the navy!" Chogan shouted with a chuckle that Santha echoed.

"We all have orders. The Soul Collector is just following his. If we catch up to them in less than a day's time, all will be forgiven," Santha interjected. Chogan looked around at the state of their boat.

"We lost almost all of our provisions. We need to get out of these clothes to dry them, and we have not one source of fire. We have barely enough water to make the

223

night through and no food. Amaro, can you tell where we are yet?" Chogan demanded in an uneasy voice.

Santha squinted through the foggy lens of his looking glass. "Blast this thing!" he cried.

"Let me try it," offered Amaro. The young charter took the looking glass and strained his focus through it. "I think I see land ahead. It is all dark and uninhabited looking. If I had to guess, it looks very much like Caaroucaëra," Amaro said excitedly. Chogan groaned.

"Great, just what we need. The only people who ever go there are cannibals from the isle of Basseterre. All of the nearby ports in the area are governed by French authority. We cannot risk either, which means we are a long way from new supplies," Chogan stated in a tone of disappointment.

"Wait a minute," said Santha. "Amaro, you once told the crew a tale regarding the island of Aichi. Is there any truth to what you said?" the captain asked.

"You mean the fortune tellers?" Amaro inquired in reply. Santha cautiously nodded. "It is true as far as I know. The man who told me the story is trustworthy," Amaro said proudly.

"What tale was this? I must have missed it," added Chogan.

"There is a little tavern of sorts on the island of Aichi. According to Amaro's friend, the women there run a fortune telling business. But for the right price, they offer *other* services as well," Santha answered with a crooked grin.

"You mean?" Chogan's inquiring eyes lit up.

"Rum and whores," Amaro answered with a laugh.

Chogan loudly slapped his left hand on the helm and howled.

"Don't get too excited. We will have to sneak onto the island. There is a big navy fort near the harbor we must avoid. By the time we see the island, it should be easy enough to land right on the beach, out of sight. Let us hope the women are still awake. It is past midnight by now," said Amaro.

"Once we have some well deserved fun with the women and gather new supplies, we will have to work in shifts to catch up to the *Unda Jaulaor*. But if we all agree to do this, we have to keep it a secret. Do we all agree?" Santha asked with a grin.

"Aye!" yelled Chogan.

"Aye! It will be worth it. I promise," Amaro added with a smile.

The condition of their catboat did not allow for the most expeditious sailing. It took the men roughly two hours to reach Aichi and cast ashore.

"We must travel light and quiet. I have no idea how well patrolled this island is. An off hand encounter with the local lawmen could only end badly. Stick together. Places like this are often homes to highwaymen, " Santha warned, as he grunted to pull the catboat up the sand.

"You know the way?" Chogan asked.

"I remember the story like it was told to me this morning. I will lead us the way my friend had described," replied Amaro.

The three men trekked across rolling sand dunes and low growing bushes, well away from the port town of Vieux Fort. They were eager, but careful enough to remain undetected. They carried only their money, and the desires of men who had been out at sea for months.

Roughly half an hour after landing, they arrived at a clearing on the outskirts of town. Amaro silently halted his comrades with the wave of his hand. A few burning lanterns dotted the town's center, but overall the land was nearly dark.

"I think I see it up ahead," Amaro whispered.

"It looks closed," Chogan quietly sighed.

"Places like that never close. That is why they keep their business so far from town. We may as well keep going," countered Santha.

The remainder of the walk was longer than it looked. Halfway across the meadow, they found a well worn road leading up a gradual slope to the sacellum. By the time the three sailors reached the pathway that led to the building's front porch, they could no longer see the town itself. Only little specks of lantern light remained visible through the trees in the distance. Immediately behind the sacellum, there grew a thick and untamed forest that had gone eerily silent for the night.

Inside the sacellum, Nerea was sleeping in the rear bedroom. Across the hall, Nakos was asleep in his own room. He was the personal assistant to The Order of the Third Eye, and the only permanent resident of the sacellum. Nakos was not gifted with clairvoyance like the members of the order, but he would always wake at the slightest sound. He only needed to hear the wooden gate lightly bang out front to immediately sit up in his oversized cot. He turned his head and continued to listen. Then, a series of soft knocks came at the front door.

Nakos brushed his long graying hair away from his eyes and swung his stilt like legs out over the floor boards. He was a mixed native islander. When he stood up straight, he was nearly six and a half feet tall, but no more than 190 pounds soaking wet. His face was narrow and clean shaven while his golden brown eyes were large and protruding.

The women liked having Nakos as their assistant. He was smart and polite, and having a man on the grounds offered them some way of protection. His height alone was a deterrent to most troublemakers. Though some people found him intimidating, in reality he had the disposition of a librarian monk.

"Visitors at this hour?" Nakos whispered as he tip toed into Nerea's room. Nakos gently shook her nearest shoulder.

"My lady, a knock just came at the door," he announced in a carefully hushed voice. Nerea whimpered and rolled over at first, but then her eyes shot open and she sat up.

"Who could be here at this time of night?" she asked, paying less mind to her voice than Nakos.

"I heard at least two pairs of feet on the porch. None of Lady Yoana's customers ever come around this late. We should leave the door barred," Nakos quietly suggested.

"No, it could be Pieter, the one Yoana said would come this way. He is unfamiliar with our customs. I will get dressed. Stay out of view, but close enough to listen." Nakos nodded reluctantly and stepped out of her room.

Nerea quickly made herself as presentable as she could. Another series of knocks came, but louder.

"Coming!" she called across the main room.

She stopped to light a candle at the back of the room, and one more on the round table towards the center. Nerea stopped just short of the door.

"Who calls at this hour?" she asked through the door. She could hear faint whispering, and then a series of giggles.

"Shouldn't you know?" a voice inquired in return. Nerea listened carefully.

"We have money. But now we are all wondering if we should spend it here. We thought that fortune tellers had foresight!" The voice sounded somewhat familiar to Nerea, so she began to unlock the door.

"Raxka, is that you?" she asked just as she swung the door inward. Santha boldly stepped through the opening first.

"No. There is no *Raxka* here," Chogan answered as he strolled in with Amaro right behind him. Nerea turned her face to hide her shock. She had never seen a member of Mortifer's navy up close, but she had heard enough descriptions of their attire to be certain of her new guests' identity at a glance. Once she gained back some modicum of composure, Nerea turned to the men with a smile.

"How may I be of service at this very early hour?" she asked in a delighted tone that belied her swollen apprehension. Chogan and Amaro giggled at one another, like young boys pulling a prank.

"Service, an apt word for why we came," Santha smoothly answered with a twisted grin. Nerea did not understand the inference in the tiniest way.

"Something to drink before we begin?" she asked. The three men all simultaneously slapped a silver piece on the

228

table, as if they had rehearsed the motion a hundred times before.

"Rum!" the men clamored together, followed by yet another dose of snickering.

"Rum it is," Nerea answered cautiously, and then walked toward the back of the room. She ducked into the hall in a near state of panic.

"Please tell me..." she began, in a nearly inaudible whisper.

Nakos made a shushing sign with his left hand and produced an unopened bottle of rum with his right. Nerea looked back at him in complete surprise.

"I am allowed," Nakos whispered with a shrug.

"I do not think these men came to hear a reading," said Nerea. She whispered so low, she had to lean close to Nakos' ear to ensure that he heard her.

Nakos made a motion around his chest and then tugged at his shirt.

"The uniforms, I know," Nerea commented. Nakos softly turned her head to whisper in return.

"Mortifer's navy, no doubt. They think this is a bagnio." Nerea's eyes froze open. She made a panicked motion with her hands as if asking, *how?*

"Who knows where they got the notion? Likely the churlish rumor of young men who like to brag about having women they never did. What I can tell, by their demeanor and comments, they expect harlotry. You are the only woman here. We should not have opened the door," Nakos added with a half hearted shake of his head. Nerea appeared to be on the verge of tears.

"What is taking so long?" Chogan barked across the room.

"Go, stall them, fill them with this," Nakos quietly implored as he passed her the bottle. "I will handle it," he added with a gentle push. Nerea quickly cleared a tea set off a serving tray and replaced it with the bottle and some mugs.

"Coming!" she answered from the hall. When she strode across the room, none of the men could tell whether anything was amiss by the expression on her face.

"My apologies for the delay. I wanted to find a fresh bottle just for you," she announced while she began untwisting the wire off the cork.

"Nice!" beamed Amaro. Santha quietly stared at Nerea's ample bosom, noting how wonderfully her breasts shook behind her blouse as she struggled to remove the cork. She did not need to look up to know where the captain's eyes were hovering.

The mugs were the kind used for coffee, with no way to measure a drink. Nerea poured three oversized shots and passed them across the table to each man, one at a time. Santha eyed his mug as he lifted it.

"Nice drink for the price," he commented. Amaro raised the mug at his captain and then drank the rum in a single gulp. "Ha! Ha!" Amaro gleefully shouted. "That is good!"

Satisfied the drink was safe, both Santha and Chogan quickly downed their drinks as well. The trio repeated the same silver coin slap as before, and Nerea moved from cup to cup, filling them just a little more than the first round.

Nerea reached Santha's cup last. When she finished the pour, Santha grabbed her by the waist and jerked her onto his lap.

"So... How do we get to the... extra services," Santha asked as he ran the back of his hand up Nerea's sleeve. It took every last bit of her restraint to keep from recoiling at his touch.

"First, you have to buy a minimum of three drinks. Then, if you are worthy, you will have a reading." Nerea attempted to sound alluring in her reply, though she could barely tolerate where she was seated.

"There is always some manner of corkage at these places," Santha commented with a sarcastic head shake. Chogan and Amaro began to chuckle.

"I can perform a reading on all three of you for one price," Nerea returned.

"Sounds good!" Chogan happily cried. When Santha's hand slithered across her right breast, Nerea gently turned away and stood up from his lap.

"Now, now, I am the madam of the house. You will have to wait for the girls to come. Drinks first, then the reading." Nerea confidently gave the men a flirtatious wink. In return, they all downed their drinks in one swallow.

"See, I told you I heard whispers when we first knocked. She was getting the girls up and ready," Chogan, concluded with a wink to Amaro.

"I am sad to hear that you are not among the choices. I was looking forward to knowing *all* your talents," Santha said with a laugh.

"If you have any money left, and the will after my girls are through with you, we can talk then," Nerea boldly replied. Chogan and Amaro both whooped and hollered as they slapped two more silver coins on the table in unison. Santha was beginning to look both groggy and wary.

"Oh what the hell," Santha calmly slurred, and then slapped his own silver piece on the table.

Nerea casually circled the table, refilling the mugs, taking care that the bottle did not go empty before she got back to Santha.

"This is really good rum," Amaro blurted out. Chogan raised his mug into the air and cried "Aye!" With their attention distracted, Nerea turned away just long enough to unbutton her upper blouse. She placed the rum bottle on the table and took a seat across from the men. As she leaned forward, she used her upper arms to squeeze her breasts together, pushing them forward, further accentuating her already considerable cleavage.

"Take your time with the drinks, and look this way now," Nerea calmly requested. When the trio looked across the table, it took only a fraction of a second for them to become captivated by the beauty of her golden brown skin exposed by the candlelight.

"I know sailors when I see them, but I have never seen such handsome uniforms. From what navy do you hail?" she asked in a tone of playful curiosity. Santha quietly stared at her chest, unable to make any reply. Chogan and Amaro both quietly laughed at their captain.

"You are not French, definitely not British, so I am going to guess, Italian?" she continued. Chogan and Amaro broke into a continuous stream of giggles.

"I tell yin! I tell yin!" said Amaro, loudly mimicking her through his laughter.

"I tell yin has a nice pair o' bosoms!" Chogan added excitedly while poking at Amaro with his elbow. Nerea forced a smile at the remark as best as she could.

"Yes, Italian," Santha answered with a silly looking, half drunken grin.

"Italians. You have come a long way then. You are looking for something here in the islands," Nerea continued, her voice growing ever more seductive.

Chogan and Amaro looked at Santha for guidance. Their captain was still deadlocked in a staring contest with the outline of Nerea's nipples as they poked through the fabric of her blouse.

"Our *boss* is looking for some old shaman that some say is dead." Chogan was slurring his words even worse than before.

"I thought it was the guy we were after. Oh wait," said Amaro, through equally slurred speech. Chogan half heartedly smacked him in the back of the head.

Nerea's entire body froze at the proclamation. For a moment, she was afraid she might have given herself away.

"The shaman is the guy. The guy is the shaman, you fool." Chogan shook his head and looked to Nerea. Then he burst into an uncontrollable string of laughter once more.

Nerea instantly knew that 'the shaman' really meant Peiman. But she could not tell if Amaro had an unintended slip of the brain, if his understanding of *the guy* was actually Pieter.

"Go on," Nerea beckoned them in an inviting tone.

"Speaking of dead, our boss probably thinks we are too," Amaro snickered. Chogan waived a finger at his younger ship mate.

"That is right. Madam, you have to promise not to tell anyone we were here. We got separated from our group, nearly sank at sea in fact. Our boss would kill us for being here and not being dead," Chogan added.

"Even if the Italian admiral himself should come here, your secret is safe. I promise," Nerea assured them. Chogan and Amaro laughed yet again at the word 'Italian.'

"She is *good*. So good, and *so* very fine," said a wobbly Santha.

"Your commanding officer thinks you are dead because of the terrible storm we had earlier. How awful. You must be in need of supplies. I can set you up before you depart. No worries," Nerea said with a double edged grin.

"Our boat is just south of here. We will need some lumber and canvas for repairs," Amaro added as he nursed his drink.

"Enough talking. Where are the girls?" Santha asked impatiently. He had not touched his third drink yet, and was beginning to sound like the alcohol was slightly losing its grip. Nerea's mouth suddenly went dry. She had expected a sign of some kind or another from Nakos long before the question came up. Just as Nerea was formulating something else to say, the front door suddenly swung open.

"Hello boys," called a female voice from the front yard. "Come out and play by the fire we have made for you," the voice added. Nerea did not immediately recognize the voice. She did not need another cue to rise from her seat either.

"Ask and you shall receive," Nerea stated as she made for the door.

"Outside? A fire?" Amaro asked as he stumbled to his feet. Chogan gulped down the rest of his drink.

"Come on! They mean for us to be like heathens, hot and sweaty!" Chogan said excitedly. He could barely walk the fifteen feet to the door in a straight line. Amaro finished his drink and stumbled out the door behind Chogan.

Santha eyed the cup of rum on the table and decided against having it. He moved his hand to the table, as if he was considering whether to take back one of the coins, but then changed his mind. He turned to the door, half expecting to see Nerea still standing on the inside of it, but she was gone. His legs were still on the wobbly side, but he got up and did his best to catch up to his shipmates.

Once outside, Santha saw Nerea and another young woman leading Chogan and Amaro around the back of the sacellum. Santha doubled his speed. Then he saw that Chogan and Amaro had stopped while Nerea and the young woman continued on. Having gained some separation, and recognition of the other young woman, Nerea leaned over to listen her.

"Nakos brought Raxka's archers. We just need to keep the sailors at a distance, but distracted." The young woman went by the name of Aylen. She was around twenty, thin and pretty, with shoulder length brown hair, and dark bronze skin.

Just beyond the fire were two more women, Rayen and Tamaya. Both were around the same age as Aylen, a little bit taller and fuller figured, but with pleasing facial features to match their shiny black hair. Nerea was surprised to see them dancing by the fire and laughing playfully, wrapped only in blankets that barely covered their naked forms.

Nerea quickly scanned the surrounding tree line. There was no sign of Nakos or anyone else he may have brought.

"Are you sure this is a good idea Aylen?" Nerea quietly asked. Aylen confirmed with a nodding of her eyes.

Chogan and Amaro remained frozen and stared. They had drank so much, they had to lean on one another for support. Santha briskly turned the corner, almost angrily, but he immediately relaxed at the sight of Rayen and Tamaya.

"Like heathens, hot and sweaty," Amaro said in a voice laden with desire. Santha's eyes scanned from side to side with a skeptical glare.

"Stay back," he ordered.

"Huh?" muttered Chogan.

Rayen and Tamaya both began to let their bare breasts slip out of the blankets for tiny half seconds as they danced seductively behind the fire. Amaro could feel himself growing aroused and began to unfasten his belt.

"You cannot back out now, Captain!" Chogan bellowed with a grin.

"I want to see the madam undress," Santha announced. Nerea quickly looked to Aylen.

"I do not want him to touch me," Nerea growled through a whisper.

"Just play along, in case he suspects," Aylen quietly encouraged. Nerea's groan was nearly inaudible as she turned to face the three sailors.

Nerea swung her hips enticingly, dancing to the same silent song as Rayen and Tamaya, and slowly removed her blouse. She crossed her arms over her head and began to shake her wonderfully large and bare breasts in the meandering light of the fire. Chogan let out another of his lustful, boyish howls at the sight.

Rayen and Tamaya both dropped their blankets to the ground, exposing their bodies completely.

"Now it is our turn to watch you undress," Aylen suggested in a most provocative tone. Chogan began to pull off his fatigue shirt when Santha motioned for him to stop.

"Not before the madam takes it *all* off," Santha said loudly. Nerea slowly turned around and lowered her hands to her hips.

"Why don't they shoot?" she whispered angrily, as she began to slide her skirt down around her backside.

The three men began to clamor in excitement at the sight of Nerea's perfectly full buttocks.

"Pretend with me," Aylen offered nervously.

"Better you than them," Nerea whispered back.

She had some sense of what was to come when Aylen shed her top and dropped to her knees.

Aylen moved her face in close to Nerea's full, but well manicured pubic region, and began to make exaggerated up and down motions with her head. Though Aylen was not actually touching her, Nerea could still feel her breath, and began to moan convincingly enough.

Santha, Chogan, and Amaro genuinely believed that Aylen was making oral love to Nerea, and just stood there in a silent combination of admiration, curiosity, and desire. Santha finally began to loosen his belt.

"If I do not have one of them right now I am going to explode!" Amaro said loudly, right as he began tearing the fatigues from his frame. Chogan was so drunk, he struggled just to unclasp the buckle on his belt, but figured it out soon enough. Santha tossed his fatigue top aside but did not remove his pants. He was determined to have Nerea, whether she agreed or not.

Santha quickly advanced toward the fireplace when he felt a piercing sting in his shoulder. By the time he recognized the feather flights on the shaft protruding beneath his collar bone, another arrow struck him in between the ribs, right over his heart.

Santha dropped to his knees in writhing pain, unable to breathe. Amaro heard his captain's loud grunt and turned to look. As soon as he saw what happened to Santha, Amaro felt the same burning pain in his own breast. A horrified look came over Amaro's face when he looked down at the arrow lodged deep in his chest.

"Chogan!" Amaro cried, just as another arrow punched through his ribs.

Chogan had just stumbled out of his pants when he heard an arrow whiz past his ear, striking loudly on the rear wall of the sacellum behind him. Once he saw Amaro drop to the ground, Chogan realized what was happening. A second arrow clipped him in the arm as he spun away and ran around the corner of the building.

It happened so quickly, that Nerea did not realize the archers had even fired until Chogan shrieked. She quickly gathered her clothes as the other young women got dressed.

"The loud one, he is getting away!" Nerea announced. Just as the words left her mouth, the archer known as Raxka unleashed his brindle Dogo Canario, a huge mastiff like dog the Spanish commonly employed to catch large game.

Chogan cursed the rum through his panting as he clumsily ran bare naked across the front yard toward the meadow. Blood ran down his upper left arm where the streaking arrowhead had nicked him. His injured right arm began to ache right through the alcohol that had temporarily stopped it from throbbing.

He half expected to hear voices, gunfire, anything. But the air was strangely still and quiet. Only when his own footsteps slowed did he hear the heavy paws of the Dogo Canario closing in from behind. True to the breed, the dog never barked or even growled before it leapt.

"No! No!" Chogan cried rapidly, just an instant before the dog sank its fangs into his injured arm. The massive dog easily pulled Chogan to the ground and began shaking its head with Chogan's arm clamped in its powerful jaws. Chogan could feel the bones of his forearm popping and

239

splintering. He wanted to wail in pain but his whole body froze in shock. Then came a whistle and the dog released its bite.

Before Chogan could make a sound, Raxka moved in from behind with a short length of sturdy twine. Chogan had no time to react to the cord going around his neck. He just felt the immediate tightening of it. Chogan clawed at the twine once or twice, and tried to stand up, even as his bladder emptied uncontrollably. Chogan's vision quickly faded to black, and then went out altogether.

Raxka tightly held the twine for a good few minutes after Chogan's dying spasms ended. Once he was sure the sailor was dead, he dropped the body right where it lay. Raxka snapped his fingers at the dog and together they sprinted back to the rear of the sacellum.

Nakos was busy rooting through the dead sailors' pockets while the women finished making themselves as decent as they typically would be. Two more archers walked about and collected their spent arrows.

"Did you enjoy your little show?" Nerea asked sarcastically, but with a hint of embarrassment too. Nakos looked up from his task with a semi confused face.

"I would have spared you that humbling experience. The goal was to get the sailors out of their clothes, not you," Nakos replied apologetically.

"Why?" Nerea asked.

"Raxka told the other girls to do their best to distract them, and convince the three sailors to get totally naked." Nakos nodded toward the lead archer who had just returned with his dog.

Raxka was a thirty-five year old native islander. He was powerfully built, bulging with huge muscles like his dog, and just shy of six feet. He had a smooth and narrow face, black hair, and eyes like obsidian rock. He was of mixed Spanish and native heritage, quite handsome, and among his most guarded secrets was his attraction to Nerea.

"I came because you were in danger," Raxka began. "We did not know if Mortifer's men were armed. It was the only way to be sure of your safety. They could have had knives or pistols in their pockets. Like that one," Raxka stated with a forward nod. Nakos held up a wicked looking dagger that had been concealed sideways behind Amaro's belt.

"It also made any escape attempt more difficult for them," said Nakos as he tossed the dagger aside.

Nerea covered her mouth when she looked at Amaro's corpse. She had never witnessed a man's death by the hand of another man. Wanting to cry, Nerea took a deep breath, and tried to regain her normally steady composure.

"We have to erase any trace of them," she said somberly.

"Their master may come looking for them anyway," Nakos interjected. Nerea shook her head.

"Once the rum started to take hold, the younger two began spouting off at the mouth. They told me they were part of a bigger group of ships and became separated. Their master thinks they are dead, lost to the sea in that storm yesterday. They also said they beached their boat just south of the meadow. We need to do something with it. If we remove all evidence they were here, no one will ever know." Nerea looked to Nakos, who then looked to Raxka.

"Throw their clothes in the fire. Burn them completely. Send the girls home. I will get my men to assist me with the bodies. We will pile them into the boat, cut their bellies open, and fill the bodies with stones. Then we will fill the boat with as many rocks as we can before it becomes too heavy to float. I will take their boat out over the reef and scuttle it. If we sink it over the reef, nothing will ever come up. The creatures of the reef will swallow it all, even the wood in the boat," Raxka calmly instructed.

Nakos looked to the sky. "It is past three by now. We must move quickly if we are to keep what happened here a secret," Nakos added in a tone of urgency.

Nerea walked over to Aylen, Rayen, and Tamaya, and hugged each one of them in turn.

"Thank you for coming here at my time of need. And thank you for going along with this unusual discomfiture. I am sorry it happened, and that you had to be any part of this," Nerea said remorsefully.

"I am not ashamed. To help a member of The Seer's order, I would do it again," Aylen answered with a smile.

"Go home, sleep, and please never mention this to anyone who was not here tonight," Nerea added. The three younger women all nodded in agreement, and then departed for their homes.

Raxka and his two archers each took a corpse over their shoulders and began walking as best they could over the meadow toward the sea. Nakos and Nerea piled the black cotton uniforms onto the fire. Nakos also tossed a few additional pieces of wood on top, just for good measure.

"The captain had a good sack of coins on him," said Nakos, pointing to it on the ground.

"Get it, and the money they left on the table. Yoana will want none of it. That is blood money," Nerea replied with a shiver. Nakos nodded.

"I know of an orphanage in Les Gosier across the strait. Mortifer is the main reason why so many of those children are there. It only seems fitting to bring them the same money paid to the kind of men who killed their parents," said Nakos.

"Yes, Nakos, you should do that. Get all of the sailor's effects that cannot be burned and bag them up. We should throw them in the boat before Raxka sinks it. Let us cleanse this place as best we can and finish what we must. We both need sleep."

Nerea went inside and quickly tidied up. Nakos grabbed the sailors' boots, belts, knives, anything that would not burn up entirely, and stuffed them in a burlap sack. Together they hurried across the meadow, toward the rolling dunes, and arrived at the beach just as Raxka and his men had finished prepping the dead bodies.

"Good, more hands," said Raxka when he saw the pair approaching. Nakos tossed the burlap bag into the boat. Santha, Chogan, and Amaro were hardly visible, but Nakos could smell the blood dripping from their torsos.

After weighing them down with rocks, Raxka and his men had placed heavier stones over top of the bodies, leaving only their heads and feet somewhat exposed. Raxka nodded at his men, and together they heaved against the catboat. Nakos moved up to the bow and began pushing with all of his might. Four men could barely move it at first. But once the keel reached the water's edge, it began to move much easier in the slippery wet sand. Further out, the catboat hung low in the water, but not low enough for Raxka's liking.

"More rocks," Raxka stated. Nakos and the two archers nodded and made haste to fulfill the request while Raxka stayed in the surf with the boat.

Nerea took a seat in the soft white sand. A peaceful breeze gently feathered her hair while the slow rolling waves broke over in solemn repetition. She could not help herself from replaying the events in the sacellum. She examined every word the enemy sailors uttered and wondered.

How could I not know of their coming in advance? she wondered. The susurration of the ocean and its pillow like draft continued to wash over her without answering her. *Was this the other event Yoana saw coming?*

Soon, Raxka was sailing the stone laden catboat away from land while his two fellow archers followed him in a dugout. It would be some time before they reached the reef, punched a hole in the catboat, and then rowed back to land. Nakos sat down on the sand next to Nerea and quietly stared forward with her.

"I never thought the day would come where blood was spilled on the grounds of the sacellum," Nerea stated, with her eyes fixed upon the sea. Nakos remained quiet, unsure of how to respond.

"We are supposed to be the peaceful ones, Nakos. We are supposed to enlighten the world with truth and hope, not darken it with trickery and violence. Tonight we became exactly what we claim to detest." Nakos crossed his arms and stretched his long neck.

"Those men were the enemy. Do not forget what that means, Nerea. They would have raped you, one at a time, maybe even murdered you, had Raxka and your friends not intervened. We are not like those we detest. We did nothing to bring those men here or deserve their intent. We stopped them from doing... goodness knows what. For all we know, we just might have saved Peiman."

"Or Pieter," Nerea added. "It worries me that Yoana is out there on the high seas. Those men told me they were part of a larger group. What if their *boss* catches up to Yoana? With Azura watching, I cannot call out through the continuum and warn our lady. We can only pray she makes it to Camahogne safely."

The smile spreading on Nakos' face seemed out of place among Nerea's comments.

"The Seer left a good six hours ahead of Mortifer's men reaching here. If there are other boats out there, and they came from the direction of the storm, they will never catch her. Have faith, Nerea."

"I do," she answered with a nervous smile. Just then, a shooting star crossed the indigo sky. It was followed by another, and then another.

"It is the Cimmerian Rising," Nerea quietly added as she watched the streaking comets. Nakos turned his head, perplexed. "The what?" he asked.

"The Cimmerian Rising, something Yoana spoke of once, quite some time ago. She was quoting the words of Peiman. It was a part of the lost prophecy. When the Primeval Scourges of the continuum fully stretch their legs and rise defiantly against the Primordial Guardians of light, stars begin to fall, and a great darkness follows wherever the fallen stars strike the land. *Men and women become unlike themselves,* she had said. It is beginning. In fact, it already began, with us, tonight. I do not remember the rest. I do not know where our place is, or what to do."

Far out over the reef, they could just barely hear as Raxka began hacking away at the catboat's inner hull with a heavy axe. His silhouette was almost invisible.

"I had never heard of that phrase until now. I will have to ask our lady, The Seer, to explain it to me when she returns. As for our place, we must be patient. Peiman will know what to do." Nakos sounded confident and very much at ease.

"Stay here a while with me," Nerea kindly requested. Nakos nodded once. "If this really is the Cimmerian Rising, then before I become unlike myself, I want to see another sunrise. I want to see its golden rays and feel the great embrace of a new morning's warmth before I become unfit to care anymore." He didn't know why, but Nakos found her statement mildly humorous, and grinned kindly at her in return.

The sky was beginning to lighten just a little. Tiny strands of gold and orange crawled along the faintest whispers of high morning clouds. Nakos concentrated on the men rowing back to shore, satisfied enough that all three were returning safely.

Nerea leaned her head against his upper arm, and watched the horizon further out. She was longing for the sun to rise up above the ocean's edge. Instead, her eyes quietly closed and she slipped into a peaceful sleep, just as the mast of the sinking catboat vanished beneath the ocean's watery furrows.

INTERMISIÓN

(TO BE CONTINUED)

HERSCHEL-FLOYD PUBLICATIONS
P.O. BOX 18067
PITTSBURGH, PA 15236

E T E R N I D A D

CIMMERIAN RISING

Original Story By B.Thomas Harwood
Copyright © 2012-2013
www.facebook.com/WorldOfEternidad

Cover Art By Kyle Anderson
www.kyleanderson.com

CPSIA information can be obtained at www.ICGtesting.com
Printed in the USA
LVOW12s0953251113

362724LV00001B/165/P